LARGE
PRINT

Melinda Hammond currently lives in a Pennine farmhouse with her husband, three children and a dog.

THE HIGHCLOUGH LADY

Governess Verity Shore longs for a little
adventure, but when Rafe Bannerman
arrives to carry her off to Highclough she
soon discovers that life can be a little too
exciting! An estate on the edge of the wild
Yorkshire Moors, Highclough is Verity's
inheritance, but the land is coveted, not
only by her handsome cousin Luke but
also by Rafe. With her very life in danger,
whom can she trust?

Books by Melinda Hammond
Published by The House of Ulverscroft:

SUMMER CHARADE
FORTUNE'S LADY
AUTUMN BRIDE

MELINDA HAMMOND

THE HIGHCLOUGH LADY

Complete and Unabridged

ULVERSCROFT
Leicester

First published in Great Britain in 2004 by
Robert Hale Limited
London

First Large Print Edition
published 2005
by arrangement with
Robert Hale Limited
London

British Library CIP Data

Hammond, Melinda
    The Highclough lady.—Large print ed.—
Ulverscroft large print series: romance
1. Yorkshire (England)—Fiction
2. Love stories 3. Large type books
I. Title
823.9′14 [F]

ISBN 1–84395–922–4

Published by
F. A. Thorpe (Publishing)
Anstey, Leicestershire

Set by Words & Graphics Ltd.
Anstey, Leicestershire
Printed and bound in Great Britain by
T. J. International Ltd., Padstow, Cornwall

This book is printed on acid-free paper

1

Miss Verity Shore did not believe in fairy tales, or in knights in armour, but sometimes, just sometimes, she yearned for a little excitement to leaven her humdrum existence as a governess. Gazing out of the window at the grey November sky, she reflected that even the weather had let her down, for the threatened snow had not arrived to brighten a rather dreary day. Shaking off such melancholy thoughts, she turned back to look around the schoolroom, wondering anew at the disorder two lively children could create in such a short time. The blazing fire threw a cosy glow over the room, although the shadows were deepening quickly as the short winter day drew to its close. She scooped up the books from the table and returned them to the shelf, pushed slates and chalks into a drawer then paused again at the window to look out at the houses clustered in the valley below. Cromford: Sir Richard Arkwright's vision brought to life. Even after a decade of building the whole area was grey with the dust from the on-going work, the vast mills and sturdy houses for the workers, as well as the excavations for the new canal. With so much labour required it was no wonder many families were flocking to the village. Not that her employer was interested in such industry: Sir Toby Hucklow considered himself too much of a gentleman to acknowledge any connection with trade, even though much of his own wealth came from the quarries that provided the creamy-grey building stone.

★ ★ ★

Miss Shore was kneeling on the floor, putting away the counting blocks when she heard the door open. She looked up.

'Sir Toby! Are you looking for the children? Lady Hucklow summoned them to the drawing room . . . '

'I know, I know, Miss Shore. It is *you* I have come to see.' Sir Toby strutted into the room, his burgundy-velvet frock-coat swinging as he moved.

Verity had risen to her feet and was shaking out her skirts but his words gave her pause.

'Me, sir?'

'Why, yes.' Sir Toby shook out his ruffles and gazed down at the large ruby that glinted from one stubby finger. 'I have not had the opportunity to speak to you since you arrived here, and I do like to be on the best of terms with my household!' He stepped forward until he was standing directly before her, so close that she could smell the greasy pomade on his black hair and see the tiny broken veins that gave his cheeks their ruddy appearance. Her instinct was to move away, but the solid schoolroom table was at her back. Assuming an expression of interest, she waited silently for him to continue. 'Yes, my dear. How long have you been with us now, a month, is it?'

'Two, sir.'

'As long as that! Well, well. Of course, I have been away from home for such a deal of time recently. And how are you settling in?'

'Very well, sir, thank you. Everyone is most kind, and the children are very good.' As long as one has unlimited amounts of energy to keep them amused, she added silently.

'Good, good. Is this your first post?'

'No, sir. I was governess to Lord Panbury's daughters until this summer, when the youngest joined her sisters at school. I explained this to Lady Hucklow in my letter of application.'

'Indeed? And you so young! Why, you hardly seem old enough to be out of the schoolroom yourself . . . but my wife speaks very highly of you, Miss Shore.'

Verity forced herself to meet his little black eyes.

'Lady Hucklow is most kind.'

'No, no, not kind. You have fitted in here very well. You are an ornament to the schoolroom.' He bared his teeth in a smile that reminded Verity of a wolf about to devour his prey. 'Most definitely an ornament.'

'Thank you, sir.' She tried to move aside but he reached out and caught her arm.

'Oh, don't run away from me, my dear.'

'Sir Toby, I have much to do — '

He chuckled, and the hair prickled at the back of Verity's neck.

'Nothing that can't wait, I'm sure.' He pulled her closer, until she could feel his hot breath on her cheek. 'I want only a little kiss. You need not be afraid of me.'

'I am not afraid,' she gasped, struggling to free herself, 'I am revolted!' She broke away and moved swiftly towards the door, but Sir Toby was before her. He barred her way, his yellow teeth still smiling.

'Come now, my dear. Enough of this jesting.'

'I assure you I am in earnest!' she declared, curbing her temper as she retreated behind the table.

'Faith m'dear, so am I. I like a filly with

spirit, it makes the chase so much more
. . . interesting!'

He lunged at her. Verity stepped back and
swooped to pick up the poker from the
hearth.

'Stay away, Sir Toby, or I will not answer
for the consequences!'

He paused, a slight frown appearing on his
brow.

'I think you would do well to consider your
position, Miss Shore.'

'I *am* considering it, sir, and at this
moment it seems most unfavourable!'

'You would be wise to accommodate me,
my dear. I am your employer, after all.'

Verity compressed her lips to prevent an
angry retort. Misreading her hesitation, Sir
Toby's wolfish grin reappeared.

'Well now, you are a sensible little puss.
What if I come to your room after dinner,
when we can — ah — discuss this?'

'Sir Toby, there is nothing to discuss. I am
employed here as a governess.'

'Yes, and what would you do if you were
turned off without a character?'

She stared at him. 'You would not.'

'I have no choice, if you persist in being
unreasonable.'

Verity's eyes darkened angrily, but before
she could retort the door burst open.

'Miss Shore there's a — oh lawks!' The maid stopped in the doorway, gaping at the scene.

'Well, what in damnation do you want?' demanded Sir Toby.

The girl dropped a curtsy.

'If you please, sir, th-there's a gentleman called to see Miss Shore.'

Verity put down the poker and moved swiftly towards the door.

'Thank you, Ellen. I shall come at once.' She followed the maid out of the room and hurried down the stairs, allowing a thankful sigh to escape her.

'We was wondering when the master would get round to you.' Ellen skipped down the stairs beside her. 'He's done it to us all, miss. But it ain't that bad, at least his breath don't smell! And he's generous. Always gives you a little present after he's kissed you.'

Verity shuddered. 'Well, I have no intention of letting him kiss me! Now who is this gentleman waiting to see me?'

'He didn't give his name, miss. Said it didn't make no odds, since you wouldn't know him. I've put him in the morning-room, since Lady Hucklow is entertainin' in the drawing-room.'

* * *

6

Before entering the morning-room Miss Shore paused. She was shaking from her encounter with Sir Toby, but it was anger rather than fear that made her tremble. A couple of deep breaths steadied her, but did not dispel the colour from her cheeks, nor the light of battle from her eyes as she opened the door. Candles gleamed in their wall brackets, but no fire had been kindled and the room was cold. Not that her visitor would notice, she thought, for the gentleman waiting for her had not removed a many-caped driving coat that added considerably to the width of his shoulders. The coat was a very pale grey, almost white and, as he was also a tall man, the overall impression was one of dominance in the small room. He was standing by the window, staring out at the dusk, but as she entered he turned, and bent a keen gaze upon her from beneath black brows. Verity was in no mood to dissemble and returned look for look.

'Miss Verity Shore?'

'Yes.'

'You are the daughter of Captain Charles Harcourt Shore?'

'I am.'

The gentleman relaxed a little.

'Forgive me for not sending up my card. I am Rafe Bannerman, of Eastwood.'

'Indeed? Should that mean anything to me?'

He frowned at her, his brows drawing closer together at her sharp tone.

'My lands neighbour those of Highclough, your father's family home.'

'Ah.' She sat down on a chair beside the empty hearth, indicating that he should do the same.

'You must excuse me calling upon you in this manner,' he continued, lowering his tall frame on to a chair opposite her own. 'I would normally have spoken with the mistress of the house before introducing myself, but I understand Lady Hucklow is entertaining.'

'That is so,' Verity affirmed, trying unsuccessfully to hide her impatience.

The gentleman bent another searching look at her.

'I beg your pardon, ma'am. You must be cold in here — '

'It is no matter, I am used to it,' she interrupted him. 'How may I help you?'

He was silent for a long moment, regarding her with an expression she could not read in his hard eyes. Then he said abruptly, 'I regret my mission is not a pleasant one. I have come to inform you that your Grandfather, Sir Ambrose Shore, is dead. In fact he died ten months ago, but it has taken me this long to track you down.'

'I see.'

His brows rose. 'Is that all you have to say?'

'Did you expect a display of grief? How should I feel anything for a man I have never met — one, moreover, who cut my father out of his will. I am not such a hypocrite.' She broke off, then continued in a quieter voice, 'I am sorry, that was very impolite. My father rarely mentioned him, you see, and never with affection.' She glanced at him. 'You know our history?'

'Yes. I am a friend of the family.'

'Then as a friend, my grandfather's death must have caused you sorrow. You have my sympathy. Was — was it very sudden?'

'No, he had been in poor health since the death of his elder son, Evelyn, two years earlier.'

'That would be . . . my uncle?'

'Yes. Following Evelyn's death Sir Ambrose had some idea of making amends to your father. He learned that Charles was already dead, and when he realized his own end was near, Ambrose renewed his efforts to ascertain if Charles had left a family. Subsequent enquiry eventually provided evidence of a widow, since deceased, and a child — yourself, Miss Shore. Since his death

I have continued the enquiries, and traced you to a seminary in Portsmouth. After that I once more ran into difficulty.' The corners of his mouth lifted. 'You proved most elusive, Miss Shore.'

'Not intentionally, I assure you. It was very good of you to go to such trouble, but I do not see — '

'Evelyn died without issue, Miss Shore. You are Ambrose's only grandchild, and his heir.' Mr Bannerman smiled at her disbelief. 'It is perfectly true, Miss Shore. With the exception of a few minor bequests, Ambrose has left everything to you.'

'To me?'

'Yes. Upon certain conditions.'

He thought for a moment she had not heard him, for she continued to stare into space for several moments before turning her direct gaze once more upon him.

'And the conditions?'

'That you are not married.'

'I am not.'

'And that you return to Highclough and live there until your twenty-first birthday, which, if my sources are correct, is May next year.'

'That does not seem unreasonable.'

'Good.' He rose and began drawing on his gloves. 'Let me know how soon you can give up your post here; I will arrange for a carriage to collect you. Doubtless you will need to discuss this with your employer — '

She interrupted him. 'Are you travelling by carriage today?'

'I am.'

Verity rose to her feet, her hands clasped tightly before her.

'And — and could you take me to Highclough?'

'I could; it is on my way, but — '

'Then if you can give me but twenty minutes I will go with you now.'

His brows rose and she allowed herself a little smile.

'Believe me, sir, I look upon your arrival as quite providential. I was wondering how soon I would be able to quit this house.'

'Oh? Are the children difficult?'

'Oh no, it is not the *children*.'

His hard, searching gaze rested on her face.

'The master's been making love to you, has he?'

She felt herself blushing and glared at him.

'You make it seem a very ordinary occurrence!'

'A very common one, by all accounts.' His tone was dismissive. He walked to the window and looked out into the street, where his coachman was bringing the carriage to a halt at the door of Hucklow House. 'Very well, Miss Shore, I will take you with me. But only if you can be ready in twenty minutes. I'll not keep my horses waiting longer in this wind.'

2

It was almost dark when Mr Bannerman's carriage pulled away from Hucklow House and descended into Cromford. Even as darkness fell there was plenty of activity in the village. The mills operated throughout the night, and the many windows of the huge buildings glowed with light. The taverns too were alive with light and noise as the building workers enjoyed their supper and ale after a hard day's labour. After they had passed the long black form of Masson Mill with its ranks of lighted windows, the signs of activity grew less, but when they reached Matlock Bath it began again, although in a different form, for here the road snaked between the river and the genteel houses, hotels and shops that made up this fashionable watering place. Lamps burned brightly to light the promenade for the wealthy visitors who had come to take the waters.

As the dim light penetrated the carriage, Mr Bannerman regarded his passenger. She was sitting in her corner, wrapped in a serviceable travelling cloak and shallow-crowned bonnet. Her hands were clasped tightly in her lap and a slight frown creased her brow as she looked out of the window.

'Is there anything wrong, Miss Shore?'

'I wonder if this is quite wise.'

He gave a short laugh. 'To drive off with a man you have never seen before? Definitely not! Tell me why you did it.'

She glanced across the carriage, but his face was in shadow. She sighed.

'Because I was angry. I have a temper, you see.'

'I did notice the touch of red in your hair when I first saw you.'

'My mother's legacy, as is the temper.'

'A disadvantage in a governess, I would think,' he opined gravely, and was rewarded by hearing her chuckle.

'A distinct disadvantage, sir! After Sir Toby tried to — to kiss me.' She paused, reflecting that the incident seemed so much more trivial since her companion had made light of it. 'After that, I wanted to quit the house with all speed, but I could see no practical way to do so. My savings were used to pay the coach fare here, and I did not think I could ask Sir Toby to pay me for the weeks I have worked. To leave with no money, and no references, would have been folly. And then you told me I was an heiress and offered to take me away. I was never so grateful for anything in my life!'

'Indeed? You gave me a very frosty reception.'

'Did I? That was because I was so angry at what had occurred. I am not usually so impolite.' She gave a little laugh. 'Although I was tempted to be *very* impolite to Sir Toby when he chanced upon us leaving the house! I wanted to give him such a set-down.'

'Then why didn't you? He no longer has any power over you.'

'The poor man looked so shocked and dismayed when you told him I had inherited a considerable fortune that my anger disappeared; in fact, I wanted only to laugh at him! Is it true, by the by, *have* I inherited a fortune?'

'That depends upon your extravagance, Miss Shore.'

'What, no house in London, no carriage pulled by high-stepping thoroughbreds?'

She saw the gleam of his white teeth as he grinned in the darkness.

'Is that really what you want, madam?'

'No, sir. As long as I have my independence I shall be happy.' She paused to gaze again out of the window. 'Do we travel to Highclough tonight?'

'Of course not. I have a room at the New Inn at Matlock.'

'Well, we must hope they will be able to find me a room, too.'

'That should not be a problem. I travelled here with a companion, a young man called James Marsden, but he has moved into the Greyhound at Cromford. No doubt his room is still free.'

'Oh, good. And — and is it very expensive at the inn, sir? Only . . . '

'Only you have no money,' he suggested.

'Precious little.'

'Then you must allow me to fund you.'

'Only until I can repay you!' she answered swiftly.

'Of course. I would expect no less of an independent lady!'

★ ★ ★

Arriving at the New Inn, Verity considered her travelling companion as she followed a servant up the narrow wooden stairs to her room. Rafe Bannerman was a strange gentleman. He had a blunt way of speaking, but he was not unkind, and she was more unnerved by his perception than his brusque manner. She wondered again if she had been very foolish to set off into the unknown with a complete stranger. After all, what did she know about this man, except that he was acquainted with her family? However, she was a practical young woman and reason told her that she was as safe in a public inn as she had been at Hucklow Hall. In fact, she thought wryly, probably safer.

Some thirty minutes later, Miss Shore entered the private parlour where she was to dine with Mr Bannerman, hiding her uncertainty behind a calm smile. The gentleman, she noted, had removed his driving coat to display a close-fitting coat of blue superfine and buckskins which showed his tall, athletic figure to advantage. The snowy white ruffles at his neck and wrists looked crisp and fresh and his black top-boots were gleaming and free from dust. Verity felt positively dowdy in her serviceable grey gown, and could only be thankful that she had taken the time to re-pin her hair.

'I hope I have not kept you waiting, sir?'

'Not at all.'

He escorted her to the table, where a waiter hovered, ready to serve her. She felt a little nervous, dining alone with a gentleman, but Mr Bannerman's calm manner soon put her at her ease, and by the time the waiter withdrew she felt confident enough to ask her companion how he had explained her presence to the landlord.

His black brows rose. 'I didn't explain

anything. Why should I?'

'Surely he thought my sudden appearance a little odd?'

'Perhaps, but it's no business of his.' He paused, regarding her with a disquieting gleam in his eyes. 'Are you concerned he will think you are my mistress?'

A gurgle of laughter escaped her.

'A dowdy female in a shabby gown and unfashionable bonnet? I am sure you can do better for yourself, sir!'

He frowned. 'Is that how you see yourself? You are in error, Miss Shore. You may not be dressed in the height of fashion, but there is nothing to be ashamed of in your appearance. You are every inch a lady — in fact, you have a great deal of countenance.'

Verity flushed. 'I was not looking for compliments, sir.'

'And I gave you none.'

Miss Shore turned her attention to her dinner: this man's plain speaking had made her stray from the usual forms of social conversation, and that was clearly unsafe. How much of her unease was apparent to her companion she could only guess, for he gave no sign that he noticed anything amiss.

He refilled her wineglass.

'My enquiries suggest that you left school to become a governess.'

'Yes, sir. My teachers recommended me to a family with only one daughter, a sickly child too poorly to attend school. Unfortunately she died within six months of my appointment and I was forced to find another post.'

Mr Bannerman nodded. 'I traced you to the seminary you attended, and they told me of your appointment, but I could not trace the family.'

'No, they moved from Portsmouth almost immediately after I left them. I think the memories were too much to bear . . . however, they gave me letters of introduction to Lady Panbury, whose three daughters needed a governess. I was with them for almost two years, and when the girls went off to school, I applied to Lady Hucklow.'

'Forgive me — was it really necessary for you to take such a post?'

She returned his look steadily. 'I had no other means of supporting myself.'

'It is a pity you did not apply to your grandfather.'

'I believed we were irrevocably cut off from my paternal relations.' She pushed away her plate and sat back. 'Why did you come?' she asked, intrigued. 'Surely you could have written to me.'

'I had business in the area and told Reedley, the family lawyer, that I would seek you out — he and I are executors of your grandfather's will, you see, and your trustees.' He paused as the servant appeared with fresh coffee and Verity used the interruption to consider her position.

'Do you know,' she said, when they were alone again, 'I have no idea where we are going? I was so angry with Sir Toby and eager to be gone that I gave no thought to the future.'

'Do you know nothing of your grandfather?'

'Only that he lives — lived in Yorkshire. I have always understood that when Father left to join the navy he was told he would never be allowed to return, so when he married my mother they settled in Portsmouth and all connection with the family was lost.' She paused, then added slowly, 'I believe my parents were very happy together, and never regretted their marriage. Mama's father had been a sea-captain, but she was an orphan when she met Papa, living with her cousins and they disowned her when she declared her intention to marry. There was never much money, barely enough for me to finish my education. But Father would not countenance contacting his family. Mama told me he swore he could never return to Highclough.'

'But you can?'

'I am not in a position to refuse,' she responded, in her frank way. 'Please, will you tell me something about Highclough? I know it is in Yorkshire — near Harrogate, perhaps?'

He pushed his chair back and turned slightly, stretching out his long legs towards the fire.

'Nothing so fashionable. There is a small village, Derringden, but it boasts little more than a church and a rather disreputable inn. The nearest town of any note is Halifax, which is about ten miles distant. The estate comprises a mixture of woods and farmland with the house itself sitting on the slope that lies between the deepsided valleys and the moors — the shelf, as it is called locally. The weather can be savage, but on a fine day one can ride for miles across the top of the world, following the cry of the curlews in the spring, and with only the skylark for company in summer.'

'You talk as if you love it.'

'I do. My own land borders your grandfather's acres and I grew up almost as part of the family.' He looked across at her. 'I pray you will not think too harshly of Sir Ambrose: he was a proud, stubborn man, a trait inherited by his son — your father. They would neither of them relent.'

21

Verity leaned forward. 'Will you tell me about my father? I hardly knew him, you see. To me he was the handsome hero who would return periodically from sea. At such times he would throw me up on to his shoulders and dance about the room with Mama. We were happy then, but such times were very brief.'

'I was still only a boy when Charles ran off to join the navy, but I remember that he was a fine-looking young man, and a courageous rider. He was open-handed and generous — he and Evelyn were always willing to let me, a mere schoolboy, tag along when they went shooting or fishing. When Charles had gone, Evelyn allowed me to fill his role, and we grew up to be good friends.'

'And Evelyn died two years ago?'

'Nearly three years now. A hunting accident. Broke his neck.' He rose, saying abruptly, 'If you have finished your meal it might be best to retire. I plan to reach Highclough tomorrow, so we must make an early start — before dawn. I have already despatched a rider ahead of us to warn them of your arrival.'

Verity nodded. 'Ask the Boots to rouse me: I can be ready within the hour.'

Verity acknowledged the comfort of her bed, and she was grateful that the landlady had warmed the sheets, but still it was a long time before she slept. It had been a strange day. She had moved from being a poor governess, persecuted by her employer, to an heiress. She had no idea of her likely fortune, but Rafe Bannerman's description of the estate gave her reason to believe she would be able to live in comfort. She knew a moment's panic at the thought of being mistress of a large, strange household, but reason told her there would be people to help her. The lawyer, Mr Reedley, perhaps, or even Mr Bannerman himself: he was, after all, a trustee and appeared to know Highclough very well. Verity snuggled her cheek into her hand and closed her eyes. Those were problems for later. She would worry about such matters as and when they arose.

★ ★ ★

Miss Shore was woken by a sleepy boot-boy some hours before dawn the following morning and she dressed by the light of one flickering candle. A welcome fire, coffee and a plate of bread and butter awaited her in the private parlour, where there was no sign of Mr Bannerman, but evidence that he had already broken his fast. Verity was pouring a second cup of coffee when the gentleman strode in.

'So you are up at last. Are you ready to leave?'

'Good morning, Mr Bannerman.' She spoke with studied calm, determined to remind him of his manners. 'There is more coffee — would you like me to pour a cup for you?'

'No — thank you. As soon as you are ready, madam, we should be going. We have a long journey ahead of us.'

Miss Shore sipped at the strong, dark brew while her companion hovered about the room with obvious impatience. She cast him a speculative glance.

'I bade the servant bring my bags downstairs: perhaps you would like to see them safely packed while I finish my coffee?' she suggested.

The gentleman's scowl grew blacker. He opened the door and growled an order at the waiting lackeys. Miss Shore hid her smile and turned back to finish her breakfast. A few minutes later she was ready and, throwing her travelling cloak about her shoulders, she followed Mr Bannerman into the yard. She cast a mischievous look at his stormy face.

'Because you dislike early mornings sir, you should not display your foul temper to the servants.'

'I am not in a foul temper!' he snapped,

handing her into the coach.

'Then perhaps it is the effects of too much wine last night,' she offered. 'I understand that can make gentlemen very crotchety.'

Her companion threw himself into the corner and tossed his hat on to the seat beside him.

'The only thing that irritates me in the mornings, madam, is a chattering female.'

Verity laughed. 'Very well, sir, I am sorry. I shall tease you no longer.'

★ ★ ★

To a young lady used to the discomfort of the common stage, her current mode of travel proved a pleasant change. The well-sprung travelling carriage bowled over the uneven roads, its occupants cushioned by the thickly padded seats. Verity warmed her feet on a hot brick pushed into the sheepskin that lined the floor and, wrapped in her warm cloak, she gazed out of the window into the morning darkness. The moon gave some assistance to light the road, but a line of hills to the east presented a black outline against the first grey light of dawn. However, by the time they reached Rowsley the cold, grey dawn was giving way to a rosy sunrise. Verity delighted in the pink gold light that flooded over the hills, glinting on the frosty cobwebs hanging in profusion from the few bare trees. Verity wanted to share the moment with her companion, but a glance in his direction showed her that the gentleman was leaning back against the squabs, his eyes closed. Undaunted, she settled back to enjoy the unfamiliar countryside.

★   ★   ★

They stopped to change horses at Bakewell, then the carriage climbed out of the town and through pretty villages of grey and yellow stone before ascending westwards through open farmland to the moors, where the occasional thin trail of smoke spiralling upwards from the chimney of an isolated stone farmhouse was the only sign of habitation. The coach rattled on over the well-made drovers' road and as they came around one sharp bend Verity caught her breath at the spectacular views of the valleys and peaks spread out before her, the dramatic rock formations thrown into strong relief by the low morning sun. Miss Shore gazed out enthralled at the view as the road fell away in a sweeping curve before the long drag up again on to the moors and the bleak track that carried them westwards. At

Chapel-en-le-Frith, they changed horses again and, as they set off, Mr Bannerman remarked that they should be in Manchester soon after noon, and would take lunch there.

'If you would prefer to press on, sir . . . '

'I would, of course, but you will need sustenance. To have you fainting off on me would be a damnable nuisance.'

She bridled. 'Far be it from me to inconvenience you, sir!'

'I knew you would wish to be accommodating.'

Verity blinked. Was he laughing at her?

Relaxing in his corner, Mr Bannerman watched her, a smile curving his lips.

'You have the most expressive countenance, Miss Shore. I find I can read it like a book.'

'Can you?'

'Easily. You are wondering whether to fire back at me, or if a frosty silence would serve you best.'

She laughed at that. 'Observant of you! But you have the advantage, sir, for I find I cannot understand you at all.'

'Strange. My friends tell me I am blunt to the point of rudeness.'

'You are certainly very frank, sir, but I had not considered you ill-humoured, until this morning.'

'Ah. I am not at my best in the early morning.'

'Then I pity your poor wife, sir.'

'You need not, Miss Shore. I am not married.'

'Oh.' She felt the tell-tale flush stealing over her cheeks and turned her gaze towards the wintry landscape. 'Will you tell me what I am to expect at Highclough? Is it a large establishment?' After a pause she added, 'Will I be there alone?'

'No. There is Margaret Worsthorne — she is a widow, the daughter of Sir Ambrose's only sister and has run the household for many years. Her son Luke now looks after the day-to-day running of the estate. Your grandfather left him a snug little property at Sowerby but he appears to be in no hurry to move on, and has agreed to remain at Highclough until everything is settled.'

'Oh, so I have family.'

He nodded. 'You are not entirely alone in the world. And there is something else I should mention: since your grandfather became ill, I have been heavily involved in his affairs, and have been in the habit of staying at the Hall one or two nights each week. There is considerably less to do now, but until you are in full control, my administration must continue, and if you have no objection it would be convenient for me to continue to keep a room there.'

'I have no objection to that, sir. In fact,' she added with a slight smile, 'I should be glad to have you on hand. The prospect ahead of me is a little daunting.'

'Come, Miss Shore, I thought you indomitable.'

'Headstrong might be a better word! My arrival at Highclough, almost unannounced, cannot be welcome.'

'You need have no fear on that head. Mrs Worsthorne will be delighted to see you, I have no doubt. I have often considered her situation at Highclough to be a lonely one. The house is quite isolated and in the winter months the roads are often impassable. I think she will be glad of a female companion. Besides, you are not entirely unexpected: she knew I was going in search of you and will not think it odd that I have brought you back with me.'

'Carrying all before you, Mr Bannerman?'

He grinned at her.

'In this instance, *I* was not the driving force!'

3

Their stop at Manchester was shortened by reports of bad weather ahead of them and after a hasty lunch they set off again with the coachman casting an anxious glance at the grey clouds gathering overhead. By the time they reached Rochdale the sun had disappeared behind a blanket of grey cloud that had settled over the sky and rested heavily on the surrounding hills. Verity regarded the darkening landscape with foreboding: perhaps it was the grey cloud, but the land looked so much gloomier, even the walls were darker than the whitish-grey stone she had known in Derbyshire. She watched from the shelter of the carriage as Mr Bannerman conferred with the coachman and, as he climbed in beside her, she gave him an anxious, questioning glance.

'We will press on.' Rafe Bannerman answered her unspoken question. 'There are no reports of snow ahead yet, but I have decided we should take the upland road rather than the valley route through Derringden. The road is steep and a little rough, but it will save us at least two hours' driving.

Don't worry, Miss Shore. You must not let the prospect of a little snow daunt you. Besides, it may not come until morning.'

Verity pulled her cloak about her and glanced up at the lowering sky.

'I hope you are right, sir.'

As they travelled north, the weather grew steadily colder and the first flakes of snow began to fall. Verity watched with growing unease as the road wound its way through a steep-sided valley, and the light faded to a gloomy dusk. Soon the coach pulled off the toll road and began a steady climb.

'We are on the direct road to Highclough.' Rafe Bannerman's voice cut through the darkness. 'There is little more than a mile to go now.'

As they left the shelter of the valley, the wind began to buffet the carriage, and the snow became finer, until it was hard, icy particles that rattled against the sides of the coach with each new gust of wind. Verity huddled into her cloak, listening to the storm. She tried to peer out of the window, but could see nothing in the near darkness. The road grew steeper and the coach groaned on its back springs as the horses struggled to drag it upwards. To Verity the journey seemed interminable. She had no idea how fast they were travelling but just as she had decided that they must be climbing a mountain rather than a hill, the carriage came to a halt.

'Wait here.' Rafe Bannerman jumped out, slamming the door behind him to keep out the storm. Verity sat alone in the darkness. She could just make out the sound of voices raised against the wind, then the door jerked open and she was obliged to hold her cloak tightly against the sudden icy blast. Mr Bannerman leaned in.

'John Driver says the horses can get the coach no further. The house is less than half a mile from here — do you think you can walk?'

'Of course.'

'Let me see your shoes.'

She pulled one foot from the snug sheepskin and put it forward for inspection, wrinkling her nose at the well-worn leather.

'One of the advantages of a life of a governess,' she said, a laugh in her voice, 'one's footwear is *always* serviceable!'

★   ★   ★

Mr Bannerman helped her out of the carriage, one hand clasping the brim of his hat as he shouted over his shoulder to the coachman.

'Leave it here, no one is likely to be coming

this way tonight. Get the horses to High-clough, then have some of the lads come back with the sledge for the baggage.' He turned to Verity. 'Are you ready?'

'Yes.'

She looked down at her feet: the snow was so fine there was very little on the ground, but it was building up at the sides of the road, and she could feel the icy surface beneath her boots. They set off along a rough lane. The light was nearly gone, but she could just make out the high dry-stone walls on each side. The wind swirled about, tugging at Verity's thick cloak. The lane carried on upwards, and as they crested the highest point, they were suddenly exposed to the full force of the wind and Verity gasped as the icy rain hit her cheeks like dozens of tiny blades. She gripped her hood, pulling it tightly around her face and trudged on, her head bent into the wind. The storm howled about her and she found her feet slipping on the uneven surface. Unable to look forward, she kept her eyes on the ground, just visible in the fading light, gritting her teeth against the biting cold and the icy wind that cut through the thin kid gloves, stinging her fingers.

'Here, let me help you.' She felt a strong arm about her shoulders. 'Keep your head down. I'll guide you.'

She found herself clamped firmly against Rafe Bannerman's solid figure and he marched her steadily forward. A few minutes later, the wind dropped and Verity peeped up to see that they had turned on to a sweeping drive and had reached the shelter of a building. She was aware of a large oak door being flung open and she was bundled across the threshold into an echoing stone passage. Breathing heavily, she swayed as she found herself free of the gentleman's reassuring grip. She blinked, dazed by the quiet calm of the entrance hall.

'You are safe now, Miss Shore,' Rafe Bannerman murmured, taking her hand to support her.

'Yes, thank you. I just need a moment to compose myself.'

There was a bustle at the far end of the passage and Verity stepped quickly away, pulling her hand free.

'Master Rafe we had quite given you up!' A plump, middle-aged woman hurried towards them, her black silk skirts rustling around her. 'When the snow began to fall we made sure we would not see you until the morning!'

'You should know I would not let a little snow keep me away from you, Megs!' declared Mr Bannerman, smiling. 'Let me present Miss Verity Shore to you — your cousin, Margaret Worsthorne . . . '

'Oh fie on you, Master Rafe, be done with your ceremony! Can you not see the child is quite done up?' Her kindly face creased into a smile as she looked at Verity. 'Come along into the parlour, my dear. Plenty of time to get acquainted once you are thawed out!'

'Thank you, ma'am,' began Verity, but the lady cut her short.

'Call me Megs, my child, for we are cousins, are we not?' She ushered Verity across a large galleried hall into a snug wainscoted room with a blazing fire. 'And you are little Verity, poor Charles's baby! To think of you living in Portsmouth all those years and we did not know it! Luke has not long come in and he said the weather was closing in with the roads well nigh impassable, so we thought you might put up somewhere for the night. However, I had Ditton put up a light supper in here, just in case, but, my dear, you look too exhausted even for that, so sit you down by the fire and I will find Cook and ask her to boil some milk for you, and perhaps when you are rested you will find your appetite.'

'And brandy for me, Megs, if you will,' put in Mr Bannerman.

'I will ask Ditton to send up a bottle,' said Mrs Worsthorne, bustling out of the room.

When she had gone, Verity removed her bonnet and shook out her flattened curls, then she pulled off her gloves and tried to untie the strings of her cloak.

'Let me.' Rafe Bannerman threw aside his own gloves and stepped forward to wrestle with the knot.

'My fingers are still too cold to be of use,' murmured Verity, trying not to think about the lean fingers moving so close to her cheek.

'They will soon recover.' He unfastened the strings and removed her cloak, tossing it over the back of a chair.

'I am sure they will, with such a good fire blazing in the hearth.'

Verity was glad to turn away from his disturbing presence. She knelt before the fire and stretched out her hands towards the warmth.

'Not that way!' Rafe Bannerman caught her hands and pulled her to her feet. 'You must warm them slowly: the fire will cause them to scorch and blister.' He stood close, holding her fingers between his own warm hands. Verity felt the hot blood coursing through her cheeks and was aware of an erratic heartbeat making her breathless. She dare not raise her eyes, but kept them fixed on the neat sapphire pin nestling in the folds of the gentleman's cravat.

'There. Are they warmer now?'

Receiving no reply, the gentleman's mouth curved into a smile. 'Faith, m'dear, this must be the first time I've known you lost for words!'

Verity looked up at that, the ready laughter curving her lips into a smile, but a moment later another voice spoke from the doorway.

'Trying to steal a march with the heiress, Bannerman?'

A shadow flickered briefly across Rafe Bannerman's features. He released Verity's hands and stepped back.

'Nothing so dramatic,' he replied coolly. 'Miss Shore, allow me to present Mr Luke Worsthorne to you.'

Verity cast a swift, appraising glance at the figure in the doorway. Luke Worsthorne was, she guessed, a few years younger than Mr Bannerman and almost as tall, but very different in appearance. He was classically fair, and where Rafe Bannerman's black hair was cut ruthlessly short, Luke's blond locks were brushed into a semblance of disorder and long enough to fall over his brow. He was elegantly attired in a dark-green frock-coat with a green and white striped silk waistcoat and pale breeches fastened at the knee with green ribbons that matched his striped stockings. The snowy lace at his wrists and the elaborate cravat hinted at a man of fashionable tastes, but there was nothing of the fop in his bearing, and in repose his lean face had a sober, thoughtful cast. This serious look was replaced by an attractive smile as the gentleman addressed her and, as he approached, she was struck by the deep blue of his eyes.

'How do you do, Miss Shore, or may I call you cousin? I believe our lines meet somewhere, for Sir Ambrose added your father back into the family tree at the front of the great Bible.'

'Cousin is very agreeable,' Verity returned his smile. 'I had come to think of myself as being without family.'

They were interrupted as the door opened again to admit Mrs Worsthorne followed by a stately butler.

'Here we are at last — and Ditton has brought up the brandy for you gentlemen. I am so glad you are downstairs at last, Luke, for I thought I should be obliged to fetch you!'

'No, no, Mama, but having been in the fields all day, I was happy enough to dine with friends in Derringden, but I could not appear here in all my dirt!'

Mrs Worsthorne tutted, but her mind had already moved on.

'Verity, my dear, you should be sitting down! What are you two gentlemen about, to keep the child standing? Pull up a chair for her, Master Rafe.'

Catching Verity's eye, Mr Bannerman grinned as he moved an armchair closer to the fire.

'You will soon become used to Megs's bullying ways, Miss Shore.'

'Bullying! Nay, sir, I had forgotten what it is to be cosseted.'

'Oh, child, never say so!' cried Mrs Worsthorne, hunting for her handkerchief. 'How it grieves me to think that you had been driven to such straits.'

Mr Worsthorne frowned. 'Dear ma'am, Miss Shore was a governess, not some demi-rep.'

'Luke!' His mama clapped her hands over her ears. 'How dare you use such language in this house! But no matter what you say you will not convince me that the role of governess is a suitable one for a member of this family.'

'Well, it is generally considered a genteel occupation,' put in Miss Shore. She was aware of Mr Bannerman's eyes upon her and felt her cheeks growing hot. 'However, I was extremely pleased when Mr Bannerman fetched me away.'

'A veritable knight in shining armour,' murmured Mr Worsthorne, his lip curling.

Rafe Bannerman's black brows rose. 'What a charming notion.'

Verity frowned, aware of an undercurrent of tension in the room and looked quickly at the two gentlemen. Mr Worsthorne was glaring across the room at Rafe Bannerman, who stared back, unflinching. Mrs Worsthorne made haste to fill the silence.

'Well, I vow we will make you much more comfortable here, Cousin Verity. But you have eaten nothing, child!'

Verity shook her head and gave an apologetic smile. 'In truth, ma'am, I am too tired to feel hungry.'

'Then we will get you to your bed, child. As soon as you have finished your milk I will show you to your room. Knowing how Master Rafe likes to travel I have no doubt that you have been up since dawn. I have told Ella to warm the sheets: she is the under-housemaid but a good, willing girl, and eager to improve herself. She is to wait on you until the weather improves, then, if you prefer, we can hire another maid for you in Halifax.'

Wishing the gentlemen a shy goodnight, Verity accompanied Megs back across the draughty hall and upstairs to a snug little chamber, where she was advised to ignore the wind howling outside the window and make haste to bed. Miss Shore had no difficulty in following her cousin's advice, but although her body ached from being jolted over bad roads for several hours, she lay awake for some time listening to the wind whistling through the cracks in the casement and hurling icy flakes at the window. She had never been so far north before, and she knew a moment's anxiety at being amongst strangers in this cold, unfriendly place. Then she remembered Hucklow House and a small chuckle escaped her.

'You were yearning for a little excitement,' she murmured to herself, as she snuggled further down under the covers. 'This may well be it!'

4

Miss Shore's first thought the next morning was that she did not need to get up to look after her young charges. However, a bubble of excitement forced her from her bed and she threw back the covers, snatching up a shawl to throw around her shoulders as she ran to the window, eager for her first glimpse of the grounds in daylight. Her room was in the west wing, overlooking the curving drive. The house faced north and on the western side a large ornamental pond looked black against the snow-covered lawns, while to the east the lawns ran smooth and uninterrupted as far as the boundary, where a fiery red sun was rising into a clear sky. The snow had fallen heavily overnight and a driving wind had thrown up thick drifts against the house. Looking past the wrought-iron gates at the end of the drive, Verity gazed at the snow-covered moors that rose steeply to the northern horizon, where a rocky granite outcrop interrupted the dazzling expanse of white. Verity hurried into her clothes, eager to explore her new home. The butler showed her to the morning-room and informed her in a kindly voice that Mrs Worthorne would join her shortly. Looking out of the windows, she noted that men were already scraping paths through the snow around the house, while a single horse was pulling a sledge laden with baggage along the drive towards the house.

'Good morning, Cousin Verity. I was hoping that your bags would be brought up before you awoke this morning.' Mrs Worsthorne came into the room, a warm shawl about her shoulders. 'Unfortunately the weather was too bad to venture out again last night and by this morning the snow was so thick the men had to dig themselves out before they could get to the carriage. Thankfully Master Rafe's coachman brought the horses up to the stables last night. They managed quite well once they did not have the weight of the carriage behind them. Now, perhaps you will come with me and tell me which of the bags should go to your room? Most of them will be Master Rafe's, but he is already at work in the office, and I do not like to disturb him.'

Verity followed her hostess into the hall.

'I thought it was Luke who had the running of Highclough?'

'And so he does, but your grandfather had several other properties about the country, and I understand that Sir Ambrose left his matters in something of a tangle. Master Rafe set up his office in what used to be the steward's room, leaving the estate-room free for Luke to attend to Highclough business.'

After identifying her own small bags, Verity followed Mrs Worsthorne to the dining-room, where breakfast awaited them.

'My dear ma'am, surely you cannot expect me to eat all this?' she declared, looking at the array of dishes on the buffet.

'Please, dear, call me Megs! I cannot abide ceremony and you will find little of it in this house. And no, I do not expect you to sample everything here, but Master Rafe is always up before dawn and takes nothing but a cup of coffee then, so he will soon need a substantial breakfast.'

'And Luke?'

'He, too, has been working for hours,' said that gentleman, entering the room in time to hear his name. 'Good morning, Cousin. I trust you slept well?'

'Yes, I was very comfortable, thank you.'

'The wind did not keep you awake?'

'No, I soon grew accustomed to it, but my plans for exploring the grounds will have to be curtailed, I think.'

'It would be wiser to remain indoors,' he agreed, 'at least until the main tracks are cleared.'

'If you would like it, I can show you over the house itself,' offered Mrs Worsthorne. 'But you should bring a shawl, for we only have fires in the principal rooms, and you will find the rest of the house rather cold.'

Mr Worsthorne looked up from his breakfast. 'The weather here can be very bleak, Cousin, I hope you have some warm clothes with you.'

'I shall manage, I think. But that reminds me of another matter I need to discuss.' Miss Shore laid down her knife and looked towards Mrs Worsthorne. 'I had no time to procure mourning clothes — '

'Oh that will not be necessary, my dear. Sir Ambrose has been dead for nearly twelve months already, so it will not be thought odd if you are not seen in deep mourning: the grey gown you are wearing will be perfectly acceptable I assure you, and I have several pairs of black gloves should you need them — not that we see many visitors during the winter.'

'Are the roads so bad then?'

'Abominable,' declared Mrs Worsthorne cheerfully. 'To go anywhere we must go either up or down, and that is impossible for the carriage in the snow.'

'You could walk, Mama,' put in Mr Worsthorne.

'Yes, I could, if I wanted to arrive at my destination wet to the knees and chilled through!' retorted his mama. 'It is one thing for you to stride across the fields and down into Derringden, quite another for a lady to go visiting on foot during such weather as this!'

Mr Worsthorne exchanged a merry glance with Verity, who smiled.

'It seems we must wait for better weather then, before we venture far. In the meantime, I would dearly love to see the house.'

After breakfast, the two ladies set off on a tour of the old house and by the end of the day they were on the best of terms. As Mr Bannerman had predicted, Mrs Worsthorne was happy to have a female companion in the house, and after showing Verity all the rooms and pointing out to her the main outbuildings that could be seen from the windows, they settled down to spend what was left of the day in the upper parlour, engaged in the humble task of mending torn sheets, as Verity happily informed the gentlemen when they all met at dinner.

Mr Worsthorne frowned at her admission.

'Really, is that necessary, Mama? Could you not find some more interesting occupation for our cousin?'

'The task suited me very well, I assure you.'

Verity smiled at him, her eyes twinkling. 'It allowed us to sit before a good fire and enjoy a comfortable cose.'

Mr Worsthorne looked unconvinced but Mr Bannerman interposed, 'I understand you toured the house this morning, Miss Shore. What do you think of it?'

'The interior is very handsome. I especially like the beautiful panelling in the great hall. However, arriving in the dark last night I have yet to see the outside of the building; there is a fine painting of the house on the upper landing which makes me eager to see the original.'

'And that reminds me' — Mrs Worthorne waved her fork at her son — 'the wall in the yellow bedroom is wet again. I think the snow must be getting in through the roof.'

'The chimney stonework on that side of the house is in need of attention,' nodded Luke. 'I shall attend to it as soon as the weather improves.' He looked at Verity. 'So you liked the house, Cousin?'

'Very much.'

'The interior was largely remodelled by your great-grandfather,' explained Mr Bannerman. 'He built the west wing to provide a ballroom and accommodation for his guests. He had ambitions for his family, I believe. However, the new block at the rear of the main house was the more practical of his achievements: it houses the new kitchens and servants' quarters, and the service rooms at the back of the house were turned into what is now the dining-room and the estate offices leading off the south passage. However, the great hall remains unchanged, and is part of a much earlier structure.'

'Like the east wing,' put in Mrs Worsthorne. 'Which is why the roof leaks so badly!'

'You will find that Rafe is very well informed about Highclough,' remarked Mr Worsthorne, refilling his glass.

'The house's history is constantly being revealed to me as I make sense of Sir Ambrose's affairs,' returned Mr Bannerman evenly.

'And are those affairs in a very bad way?' enquired Verity.

Mr Bannerman paused as if deciding how much to disclose.

'Sir Ambrose had neglected his estates for some years. Oh, Highclough itself is in good shape, Luke has taken care of that, but there are other farms and properties near Bradford and Leeds that have been allowed to fall into disrepair, and there are several farms where rents have not been collected or, worse, the tenant has quit and the land has been left idle. Add to that disputed titles — '

'I suppose it is useless to tell you that Reedley is quite capable of dealing with all this?' drawled Luke. 'There is no reason for you to neglect your own property.'

Verity looked up. 'Is that what you are doing, sir? Then surely — '

Mr Bannerman shrugged. 'My own estates are in good heart, never fear. But as to your point, Luke, Reedley is old, and while I agree he is very thorough, he lacks the energy to pursue some of these outstanding matters. However, it is all well in hand now, and I shall have everything ready to pass over to Miss Shore when she attains her majority.'

'But it seems unreasonable that you should put in so much of your own time for my benefit,' she argued.

Rafe Bannerman looked at her.

'Sir Ambrose was a good friend to my family, and after my father's death he became a guide and mentor to me.'

Verity flushed. 'Of course. I am sorry, I never meant to imply — '

'I promised him I would do all I could to help. But set your mind at rest, Miss Shore: my work here is finished for the present and if the weather holds, I shall go home tomorrow, and trespass no longer on your hospitality.'

The next morning Verity received the news of Mr Bannerman's departure with mixed feelings. When Ella brought her hot chocolate and informed her that the gentleman had already left, she was disappointed that he had not waited to take his leave of her, but at the same time she had been aware of a tension between Rafe and Luke Worsthorne. She hoped that with Mr Bannerman safely out of the house she would be able to get to know her new relations in a more relaxed atmosphere. She made her way to the dining-room to find both Mrs Worsthorne and her son were there before her. Luke greeted her with a smile and rose to set a chair for her.

'What plans do you have for today, Cousin?' he asked, as he resumed his seat.

'Why, none. That is, I thought I could help my cousin with the inventory she is compiling.'

He pulled a face.

'Very dull work. Walk with me instead!'

Verity glanced out of the window. The snow was still thick on the ground, a dazzling contrast to the rich, clear blue of the sky, but the main drive had been cleared.

'It is very tempting . . . '

Luke grinned. 'Then succumb to the temptation, Cousin! Have you stout boots to wear, or shall I ask Mama to lend you her pattens?'

'No need, my boots will be sufficient. If Megs can do without me?'

'Of course. In fact, I shall be pleased to see Luke take time off from the estate business. I vow I sometimes think he gives Highclough too much of his time.'

Luke poured a cup of coffee and handed it to Verity.

'So you see, Cousin, it is your duty to step out with me!'

★　★　★

The air was bracing and, as they walked down the main drive away from the house, the keen easterly wind whipped the colour into Verity's cheeks and tugged at the brown curls that had escaped from her bonnet. She looked towards the tall wrought-iron gates that stood out blackly against the white snow. Luke pulled her hand through his arm.

'No, don't look round yet. I want you to see the house from the main gates. At that distance you can appreciate the whole building.' He squeezed her hand. 'You must not be afraid to lean on me, for the path is

51

still a little slippery.'

'Thank you. How long have you lived here?'

'All my life. My father died when I was a baby, and Mama came here to look after my great uncle. Once I had finished my schooling, Sir Ambrose set me to work with his steward and when he died it seemed natural that I should take over.'

'And have you never wanted your own estate?'

He hesitated. It was only for a moment, but Verity was aware of the tension in him.

'My father's house had to be sold on his death to pay his debts.'

'Oh, Luke, I am sorry.' said Verity. 'But Sir Ambrose has left you a property, has he not? Mr Bannerman told me of it. Perhaps you think he should not have done so, but I was interested to know all I could about my grandfather and Highclough.'

'It is no secret that my great-uncle left me the estate at Sowerby. When Sir Ambrose died Rafe told me he would manage Highclough until you were in possession, but I thought I should stay here, at least until you had settled in.' He glanced down at her. 'Do you object?'

'Oh no, how could I do so? I am very glad you are here.'

'So too am I.' He stopped, smiling at her

for a moment before he turned her around on the path. 'Look. This is Highclough at its best.'

Verity caught her breath. The house stood before her in all its splendour. The winter sun had reached its height in the southern sky, and the north front of the building was in shadow, the creamy-grey stone dark against the dazzling snow that surrounded it and with a clear blue sky throwing the roofline into strong relief. Highclough was a long, low house, just two storeys high, giving the appearance of sturdiness rather than elegance. A gabled wing rose at each side of the great hall with its tall stone mullioned and transomed windows. Protruding between the hall and the western gable was the square tower of the entrance porch with heavily carved stonework surrounding the black oak door, while inset above it was a beautifully carved stone window in the form of a rose. Set back from the main building was the new west wing with a row of deep windows indicating the ballroom, and Verity tried to work out which of the smaller upstairs windows belonged to her own bedroom.

'Well, do you like it?'

'Luke, it is beautiful! Not at all as I imagined it. Quite magnificent.'

He laughed. 'I knew you would love it.

Come along, I'll show you the shrubbery.' He led the way to a walled garden on the eastern side of the house. 'We had best stop at the gate because the paths have not been cleared in here. Mama has never cared much for the garden, and it has had little attention in recent years, but I think it could be very attractive.'

Verity looked through the stone arch to the garden beyond, where straggling bushes drooped under the weight of snow. Several statues had been placed amongst the bushes and a stone bench stood against the house wall.

'It's a southern slope, and sheltered from the wind,' he continued. 'I believe it would be possible to grow most things here.'

'You have no need to convince me. I think you really love this house.'

'I have spent so many years looking after Highclough, farming these unfriendly slopes, is it any wonder that I should be attached to it?'

'Not at all. I only hope I can do as well.'

Luke looked as if he would speak, then changed his mind. After a moment he said, 'We had best be moving on. It does not do to stand too long in this chill wind. Would you like to see the stables?'

★ ★ ★

It was several days before the snow cleared sufficiently for Verity to venture out again. In the meantime the servants fetched up fresh supplies of food by sledge and indoors the ladies were kept busy turning out cupboards and attics. When Mr Bannerman returned to Highclough a week after her arrival, he emerged from his office at mid-morning to be confronted by the sight of Miss Shore dressed in a faded woollen gown and her arms full of old sheets.

He stopped, his brows raised in surprise.

'Miss Shore! I am sorry, I did not bring you here to be a housemaid.'

'I am nothing of the sort!' she laughed. 'Cousin Megs and I are clearing out the linen cupboards and these sheets are past mending, so I am on my way to the housekeeper's room to see if Mrs Ditton can make use of them.' She twinkled up at him. 'You would not believe how very righteous it makes one feel to have all the cupboards in order.'

'You are right, I would not believe it! My poor girl, I had no notion you would be so bored.'

'Oh I am not bored, truly I am not! I was merely teasing you!' She assured him. 'Megs and Luke are most attentive. We spend the

55

evenings playing at cards or conversing and there is a library full of books, and I have my needlework and sketching. But the fact is that Cousin Margaret has been longing to clear out these cupboards for many years and was never allowed to do so while my grandfather was alive — ' She broke off, an anxious look on her face.

'Perhaps, as you and Mr Reedley are executors, we should have asked you first?'

'My dear girl, I have no interest in household linen, and neither does Reedley. What does alarm me, however, is that you should be reduced to dealing with such trifling matters.'

She opened her eyes at him.

'Trifling! It is far from that, sir, as I think you would acknowledge if you were to find a hole in your sheet tonight!'

She saw the gleam of mischief in his eyes and backed away, laughing.

'Very well, Mr Bannerman, let us say no more on that head. But I will concede that I am more than ready for a distraction. What would you suggest?'

He gave her a considering look.

'Can you ride?'

'Yes.'

'Then I'll send a message to the stables. I have a few papers to tidy up and then we will ride out. Meet me in the great hall in an hour.'

★ ★ ★

It was a little under an hour when Miss Shore presented herself in the great hall attired in an old but well-fitting riding habit. She heard a door open and turned to see Luke Worsthorne coming out of the library. He was looking solemn.

'I heard Rafe giving orders to have the mare saddled. I am so sorry, Cousin. Had I known that you wanted to ride I would have suggested it sooner.'

'No, how could you know?' she said, smiling. 'I had not thought of it. Besides, until today the ground has been too hard for riding.'

'I still wish I was escorting you!' He came up to her, looking so angry that she placed one gloved hand upon his arm.

'We can ride out another time, Luke, when you are not so busy.'

He glared at her for a moment, then the anger left his face and he covered her fingers with his own. 'I should never be too busy for you, Verity.'

'I am sorry to keep you waiting, Miss Shore.' Mr Bannerman's cool voice was heard from the gallery and Verity looked up to find him looking down upon her. She nodded.

'I am ready, sir. I will meet you at the door.' With a fleeting smile at Luke she disengaged her hand and walked out of the hall.

★ ★ ★

The mare that had been saddled for Verity was overweight and sluggish, and she found herself eyeing Mr Bannerman's rangy black hunter with something akin to envy as she struggled to keep up even a sedate pace. A chuckle escaped her and she found her companion's hard eyes upon her, demanding an explanation.

'I am ashamed to say I was comparing my mount most unfavourably with yours, sir! This is most ungrateful of me, since for the past few years I have not been able to ride at all.'

'Mrs Worsthorne rides but rarely, I believe,' he observed.

'She does not ride at all if she can take the carriage!' came the frank reply. 'However, it is very good of Megs to allow me the use of her mare.' She sighed. 'I have no doubt that with regular exercise she will improve.'

They had turned on to a well-worn track, making their way up to the open ground.

Most of the snow had disappeared, but looking around Miss Shore could see large white patches where the drifts had collected against the rough walls that divided the upland pastures. She was moved to enquire where they were heading.

'I thought you might like to see Newlands — my home.' He touched his heels to the hunter's glossy flanks and the horse broke into a trot, while Verity's mount was obliged to canter to keep up.

'This is the quickest route, directly across the moors,' he said, waiting for her to come up. 'The carriage way winds down to Derringden and is much longer. On a fine day this ancient track is by far the better route. In summer you will find the packmen still use it. They call in at all the local farms, selling ribbons and trinkets, or collecting yarn to deliver to the local weavers. They may call on you towards dusk. Ambrose allowed them to bed down in the stables overnight but, of course, you may not wish to continue that practice.'

'I see no reason to change, as long as they do no harm.'

'They will cost you a meal and a little fodder for the ponies, but I have always thought it a small price to pay for the news they bring with them.'

They rode on, their path curving around a rocky outcrop that Verity had noticed from the great hall window at Highclough.

'Oh, what is that?' She pointed to several huge weather-worn stones that stood like sentinels at the entrance to a large circular area cut into the rock.

'It's a delph, an ancient quarry. This area is known as Bridestones. Years ago, couples used to come up here to marry — in those days it was sufficient for a man and woman to make their promises in front of witnesses to become husband and wife.'

Intrigued, Verity turned her horse off the path and rode up between the stones.

'It is sheltered from the wind here,' remarked Mr Bannerman, following her into the rocky circle.

The floor was covered with a springy turf but high stone walls sent their voices echoing back to them. Verity looked around her with interest.

'It's like a large, outdoor room!' she exclaimed. She pointed to a large rocky slab that lay beneath an overhang, forming a natural shelf.

'What is this?' she asked him, laughing. 'Some form of altar used for human sacrifices?'

He grinned. 'In a way.'

She moved the mare towards him, her face glowing with interest.

'Really? Tell me!'

'Miss Shore, such tales are not for female ears!'

Verity laughed. 'Having said so much you cannot refuse to tell me!'

'Very well. That ledge is called the marriage bed. Legend has it that couples consummated their marriage here, in view of their witnesses. That way the man could not later deny the union.'

If Mr Bannerman had hoped to shock his auditor he was disappointed.

'How barbaric!' she exclaimed. 'Uncomfortable, too. I am glad we live in more civilized times!'

Her companion laughed. 'Do you think so? I suspect this place is now used for cock-fighting and gambling.'

Verity shuddered.

'Even worse! Pray let us move on!'

They returned to the path and were soon moving down towards more sheltered farmland. Mr Bannerman stopped and raised his crop.

'There,' he said, pointing. 'That's Newlands.'

Verity looked down at the fertile valley opening out below them. The land was divided into tidy fields with lines of straight walls, and on the south-facing slope, against a back-drop of trees was a neat, square house with a regular five-bay frontage and a centre door. It was approached by a sweeping drive that curled through a well-tended park.

'Oh how pretty!'

'It is not as old as Highclough, of course.'

'But a great deal more practical!' she returned.

'I believe so.' His eyes reflected her smile. 'My grandfather built it. He intended to replace the surrounding farms with more parkland, but to date we have preferred the income from the farms. Would you care to take a closer look? We could take a little refreshment before our journey back to Highclough.'

Verity readily assented and they followed the worn path down to a wider track that eventually led them to the house itself. Mr Bannerman led the way to the stable block where a surprised groom ran out to meet them.

'Ah, Matthew. Will you take care of our horses while we step inside? Thank you. We should not be above an hour.'

He slid from his horse and walked over to lift Miss Shore down.

'Come in and meet Cook. Let us see if she

can be persuaded to provide us with a hot drink!'

He led her through a side door and along a narrow passage hung with ancient spears, shields and crossbows.

'Signs of my family's passion for the hunt,' he explained, observing her interest. 'My grandfather collected most of these trophies and insisted they should be displayed. My own preference is to take out the gun dogs for a day's shooting, although when my sister is here we set up the archery targets in the garden, or even in the great barn if the weather is too bad.'

He guided her into a large, warm kitchen, where a rosy-cheeked female in a spotless apron was dozing in a rocking chair before the fire. As the door creaked she opened one eye, sitting up with a shriek when she recognized her visitor.

'Mister Bannerman, how dare you come a-creeping up on me like that!'

'I'm sorry, Cook. Did I startle you? I have brought Miss Shore over to see Newlands, but we cannot go into the house in all our dirt.'

'No indeed, sir. Mrs Hartley would be a-scolding you for days if you was to muddy her carpets — if she was here, that is, which she isn't sir, you having given her leave to visit her sister in Leeds and saying as how you wouldn't be back again for a couple of days. Well, well, sir. Let me see what I can find for you. Coffee, is it? Or hot chocolate?'

Chattering on, Cook clattered about the kitchen, moving the kettle on to the flames and sending an open-mouthed kitchen maid to fetch the best cups for the master. Smiling, Mr Bannerman escorted Verity to the big table in the centre of the room and gently pushed her down into the armchair at its head, perching himself on the bench to one side.

'I have been in the habit of visiting Cook since I was a schoolboy,' he said. 'I hope you do not object, but having told the servants I would be at Highclough for a few days, they are most of them having a holiday, so the main rooms of the house are going to be very cold and inhospitable.'

'Not to mention incurring Mrs Hartley's wrath for muddying her carpets,' murmured Verity.

'Well, naturally, I am in constant dread of upsetting my servants.'

She laughed at that, and shook her head at him.

They were soon supplied with coffee and cake, and Verity watched and listened in some amusement as Cook continued to treat Mr

Bannerman as if he was still a schoolboy. That gentleman was very much at his ease, and when at last he suggested it was time they made their way back to Highclough, Miss Shore found herself reluctant to leave.

'How pleasant that was,' she remarked, when Mr Bannerman had thrown her up into the saddle. 'Dare I tell Cousin Margaret that I have been sitting in a gentleman's kitchen, talking to his cook?'

Mr Bannerman brought his horse alongside her. 'Perhaps not. I fear it would seriously damage her good opinion of me.'

'Hah, I don't think you care a jot for her opinion, or anyone's.'

'Now there, Miss Shore, you are wrong.' The hard eyes held hers for a moment. 'Shall we go?'

5

As November drew to a close, Mr Bannerman's visits became more infrequent and Verity found herself looking forward to the three-mile drive to the church in Derringden each Sunday, just to see fresh faces. Since Newlands was in the next parish, she knew Rafe Bannerman would not be in attendance, but Mrs Worsthorne was able to introduce her to several local families. Highclough had no near neighbours and those acquaintances they did see at church were eager to explain how difficult it was to visit Highclough in the wintertime.

'I can see that one might feel isolated here in winter,' Verity remarked to Mrs Worsthorne one evening. They were sitting in the drawing-room after dinner, and the wind could be heard howling around the house. She was surprised to observe her companion looking uncomfortable.

'It is something that has occurred to me. It has never worried *me*, of course, because I grew up here, and have never craved society. However, you might wish to consider hiring a companion.'

'A comp — but why, when I have Luke and

yourself here? Please don't think that I was complaining of being lonely.'

'No, my love, but you see, when you reach one-and-twenty the property will be handed over to you, and Luke will be moving to Sowerby. Naturally I will be going with him, so you see it might be wise to start thinking of your situation.'

'Mama, might I suggest that you are being a trifle premature?' said Luke, entering the room at that moment.

'No, I think not. After all, it is nearly Christmas, and May is not so far off.'

'No, but Cousin Verity may not wish for a companion. At least, not a female companion: she may prefer a husband.'

Verity laughed. 'That is hardly likely to happen in the next few months.'

Luke sat down beside her and fixed his blue eyes on her face. 'You think not?'

He spoke softly, but something in his tone caught Verity's attention. She sat very still, aware that her heart was thudding uncomfortably hard. She swallowed.

'I am certain of it,' she said lightly, meeting his gaze steadily.

Luke's mouth curled into a rueful smile and he gave the faintest of shrugs.

'Well, who knows? I think we need not worry about that just yet.'

★ ★ ★

The exchange nagged at Verity and she wondered if she had perhaps given Luke cause to think she would welcome a proposal from him. She hoped not, but now the idea had arisen she considered it. She was an heiress and, as such, an independent woman, but she admitted to herself that the thought of living alone at Highclough was a daunting one. However, the thought of marrying without love was even more frightening, and although she liked her cousin, she knew she did not love him, at least not yet. Verity's experience of the tender passion was limited to the romances she had read and those couples she knew. Her previous employer, Sir Toby Hucklow and his lady were not a shining example of the condition: Lady Hucklow was a cold woman, living for her society parties and her children, while Sir Toby took his pleasures in London and, as she had experienced for herself, with his staff. Verity's own parents had been very much in love, and although theirs had been an impoverished match, she remembered their affection for one another, an affection so strong that at times she felt it had even excluded her. She knew that if she was to marry, nothing less than that same overwhelming passion would suffice. This was a lowering thought, for even in the heart of a large town the possibility of meeting a gentleman like her father was remote: here on the wild moors of Yorkshire it was too unlikely to be considered.

★　★　★

A few days later, an invitation was received that gave her thoughts another turn. Mrs Worsthorne came bustling into the morning-room clutching a letter and an elegantly engraved card, which she waved at Verity.

'My love, only think! We have been invited to Newlands for the New Year Ball.'

'Newlands — Mr Bannerman's house?' Verity felt a ripple of annoyance. 'Why should he write to us, why could he not come in person? He has not been near us this past se'en-night!'

'Now, my love, you know he has his own affairs to attend to, and the days are so short now there is scarce daylight enough to ride here. But that is by the by. He has written me a very good letter, apologizing for his absence and enclosing the invitation, which is for all three of us. And he invites us all to stay overnight. Is that not kind of him? The ball has become something of an annual event in the area. Mr Bannerman's sister, Lady Winter, comes to act as his hostess. Sadly, in recent years Sir Ambrose was too ill to attend, and last year we had only just buried my poor uncle, so of course we did not go, but this year I see no difficulty. It is after all more than a year since we went into mourning, and it will be a private party. Oh you will adore Newlands, my love. Such a fine house, so elegantly furnished and with every comfort!'

'Including a good kitchen,' Verity murmured.

'What was that, love? Oh yes, I am sure the servants' rooms are in good order, but they are well out of the way of the ballroom, never fear.'

While Mrs Worsthorne eulogized, Verity fought to suppress the memory of her ride to Newlands, and the easy camaraderie she had shared with its owner. She had barely spoken to him since, proving that such a moment meant less than nothing to the gentleman. She tried to smile, and gave Mrs Worsthorne to understand that she was perfectly ready to visit Newlands.

★   ★   ★

This highlight in their social calendar gave the ladies another problem, and one that

70

could only be resolved by a visit to Halifax to buy new gowns. For Verity, this raised the vexing question of finance. She said nothing to Mrs Worsthorne, but a few days later, learning that Mr Bannerman had arrived and was working in the estate office, she decided to approach him. She knocked quietly and entered the room to find that gentleman engaged in lighting the fire. She watched silently as he carefully placed more wood on the little flame, encouraging it to grow into a crackling blaze. Satisfied, he rose, dusting his hands together.

'Oh well done, sir. What a resourceful gentleman you are!'

He swung round, a smile softening his rather severe features.

'I should have sent word. Ditton always makes sure a fire is kindled in here if he knows I am coming over. But no matter. It will soon warm up now. Did you wish to see me?'

'Yes sir. I — um — I am not sure — it is rather a delicate matter.'

'Will you not sit down, or would you prefer to go to the morning-room, where it will doubtless be warmer?'

'No, no — there is less chance of being interrupted here, I think.'

'Ah,' he said, looking down at her. 'Well?'

'You will remember, sir, that I came here with . . . very little money.'

'None, if my memory serves me correctly.'

She flushed.

'So far my needs here have been minimal, but — your ball, sir, has put me in an awkward situation.' She glanced up to find him regarding her with some amusement. Verity raised her chin.

'I have nothing to wear.'

'Indeed? My sister is forever saying the very same, yet when she comes to stay there are boxes and trunks enough to fill the house.'

Verity's eyes flashed indignantly.

'You brought me here, sir, and you know that I have come with but two small bags!'

'Why must women always be wanting a new gown? Let me reassure you, ma'am: I shall not be buying a new coat for the occasion.'

She glared at him. He was teasing her, and it did nothing to improve her temper.

'As the granddaughter of Ambrose Shore, you would not wish me to disgrace him, and the few gowns I own are none of them suitable for an assembly such as you have planned! As executor of his will, I was hoping it was in your power to release some funds for me.' Two spots of colour flushed her cheeks as she glared at Rafe Bannerman, daring him to make one more jest, for then she would leave the room and tell Mrs Worsthorne that she would not go to the ball! The gentleman met her look, and after a moment he laughed.

'Very well, I will tease you no more or you will lose your temper and rip up at me! Where will you go for your gown?'

She felt her anger subsiding.

'Margaret — Mrs Worsthorne tells me there is a first-rate modiste in Halifax.'

He took out a card and scribbled a hasty note upon the back.

'Very well, tell her to send the reckoning to me.'

She took the card.

'Thank you. You will make sure you are reimbursed out of the estate?'

'Of course.'

'And you have not forgotten that I owe you for the expenses incurred on the journey here, the charges for the inn at Matlock? That too must be paid for.'

'Oh be damned to that! Do you think I cannot afford to pay for one night's lodging?'

'I am sure you can very well afford it, but it is not right that you should.' He growled something incomprehensible and, having won her point, Verity's own demons prompted her to add, 'A new gown *is* an extravagance, sir, I know, but I thought to put it to good use.'

'Oh?'

'It occurs to me that in the new year I might attend the assemblies in Halifax, or even Leeds! To find a husband, you see.'

'I'll be damned if you will!'

She continued as if he had not spoken. 'Mrs Worsthorne is quite excited at the idea.'

'You will hardly travel to Halifax alone.'

'No, no, I am sure Luke will escort us.'

'And I'm sure he will not!'

'Well, if that is so, one of the servants shall ride with us.'

'Tell me, Miss Shore, why this sudden desire to enter society?'

'Surely you know, sir, that every young woman enjoys dancing! Besides, I have a fancy to marry.'

He frowned at her.

'By the terms of your grandfather's will you cannot do so without the consent of the executors.'

'But that is only until I am one and twenty,' she reminded him. She observed with satisfaction that he was glaring at her, his jaw clenched.

'Of course,' she continued, 'once it is known I am an heiress, I have no doubt it will be very easy to find a husband.'

'Finding a suitable one might be more difficult.'

'Oh, but suitable sounds so *dull*.'

He strode across the room and gripped her by the shoulders, glowering down at her. 'Miss Shore, if I were not an executor of that damned will — '

Her eyes widened innocently. 'Well, what would you do?' She waited expectantly.

'I would wash my hands of you, you burdensome wench! But since that is not so, let it be understood that while I am your trustee there will be no assemblies, and no talk of finding a husband.'

He let her go.

'But there might well be a suitable gentleman at your own ball.'

'Then it will be my delight to tell him you are *not* a suitable bride!'

She gave him an innocent look. 'Oh, why not?'

He towered over her. 'Miss Shore,' he ground out, 'if you value your skin you will leave this room. Now.' With a gurgle of laughter bubbling on her lips she tripped to the door, only to be stopped when he called her name again.

'Here.' He handed her a bundle of notes. 'You will no doubt be wanting gloves and stockings and a dozen other nonsensical female necessities as well as your gown.' She counted the notes.

'B-but there is a hundred pounds here!'

'Aye, so you had best make sure you can account for every penny.'

'Oh, I will!' Upon impulse she placed her hand on his shoulder and stretched up to kiss his cheek. 'Thank you, my kind and generous trustee!'

'Baggage!' he threw after her, as she left the room.

★ ★ ★

Verity was still chuckling as she closed the office door behind her. Her smile grew as she saw Luke standing by the back stairs.

'Cousin — I heard raised voices; have you been arguing with Rafe?'

'Why yes.' An irrepressible dimple appeared. 'We cannot meet without doing so.'

Luke frowned. 'You shouldn't cross him, Verity.'

'But I cannot help it when he is so unreasonable.'

'Unreasonable? Why, what have you said to upset him?'

'Nothing much, merely that I have decided to look about me for a husband!' With a bland smile, she slipped past him and made her way to her room, still laughing.

6

With the weather worsening, Mrs Worsthorne advised that they should lose no time in making their trip to Halifax. Mr Bannerman had returned to Newlands with no plans for visiting Highclough again before the New Year. Miss Shore wrote to him, suggesting that on her visit to Halifax she should contact Mr Reedley, the family lawyer and joint executor of Sir Ambrose Shore's will. She received a curt note by return, advising that she should do as she thought fit.

'Which shows, Margaret,' remarked Miss Shore, showing the note to her companion at breakfast, 'that he has not the slightest interest in my well-being. If he had any proper feeling he would have arranged to bring Mr Reedley here to see me.'

'No, no, I am sure you misjudge him,' declared Mrs Worsthorne. 'I have known Master Rafe since he was a boy and he is as kind as can be.' She hesitated, then added, 'Although he *can* be a little blunt at times. From what I know of him I have no doubt that he is already sincerely attached to you, as Sir Ambrose's heir.'

'He is certainly attached to Highclough,' put in Luke, coming into the room at that moment. He observed Verity's frown and added bitterly, 'Rafe has always been allowed to run loose here and considers himself part of the family. He rides over this estate as freely as his own.'

Mrs Worsthorne waved her hand. 'Well, and is that not to be expected, when he was such a friend of Sir Ambrose and his sons?'

Luke came to the table and sat down opposite Verity.

'With all three of them dead he can no longer have a claim on the family.'

'He is however an executor,' murmured Verity.

Luke looked across at her. 'Only until your birthday. After that you can tell him to go to the devil!'

Verity smiled at his sulky frown.

'Surely you would not have me forbid him on to the land? It is unlikely that I shall cease to need his help and advice for some time.'

'Is my advice not sufficient, then?' he threw at her.

'Luke, I did not mean that! But you have your own land now. Mr Bannerman told me you had only agreed to remain here until I come of age.'

'And do you think I would leave you here

then to manage alone?'

'Well, no, I would hope that before that time you will show me something of how the estate is run, and assist me in appointing a new manager.'

'Have you discussed this with Rafe?'

'No — '

'I wonder that he has not brought the subject up. Especially when he is so adamant that you should not marry.'

'No, no, Luke, you misunderstand! Mr Bannerman and I always rub each other up the wrong way, but there is nothing in that. I have no doubt that he will wish to discuss the management of the estate soon.'

'And your search for a husband.'

She flushed. 'It is hardly a *search*! But I am sure that if I should meet an eligible gentleman that I *truly* wished to marry, Mr Bannerman would not stand in my way.'

Mr Worsthorne looked a little sceptical, but before he could answer, his mama rose.

'I am off to the kitchens to see Cook. Luke, will you be dining with us, love?'

'No, Mama. I am riding into Derringden to meet Sam Greenwood.'

'Gambling again, Luke?' There was an anxious note in the widow's tone.

'Devil a bit, Mama! Just a game of cards with a few choice spirits. Where is the harm in it?' He rose and as he passed his mother he stooped to kiss her cheek. 'Don't fret, love. I shall be home before midnight!'

He lounged out of the room and Verity glanced up at Megs.

'You do not like his friends?'

'Like!' Megs spread her hands. 'Sam Greenwood is a lazy good-for-nothing! He is the son of a rich wool merchant and he takes Luke to clubs in Halifax where it is nothing to lose hundreds at a sitting! And as to his other friends, well, most are not fit company for a gentleman!' She shook her head, sighed, then gave Verity her brightest smile. 'Don't mind me, child, it is all nothing! A young man must have a little wildness, after all! Now, I promised Cook I would check on the grain chests for her, to make sure we have sufficient oats and barley for the rest of the winter!'

The good lady hurried away, leaving Verity to her own thoughts, which immediately returned to Luke's animosity towards Rafe Bannerman. Her cousin's insinuations haunted her: she had begun to depend upon Mr Bannerman and it disturbed her to think that he might not be working for her best interests. Her mind was somewhat put at rest after her visit to Mr Reedley. She had written to the lawyer requesting an appointment, and while Mrs Worsthorne continued with her shopping, Verity spent an hour with the lawyer in his chambers, discussing the terms of her grandfather's will. Mr Reedley had been the family lawyer for many years, and he declared that he had every confidence in Mr Bannerman, but it was clear to Miss Shore that the lawyer was nearing the end of his career and she doubted that he would question any decisions made by his co-executor unless they were truly outrageous. However, she came away from the meeting sufficiently reassured to put her doubts aside, and to enjoy the novelty of purchasing a gown for the Newlands ball.

The fashionable modiste favoured by Mrs Worsthorne turned out to be an experienced seamstress with excellent taste. She assured them the dresses could be made up in a trice, and the ladies spent a few happy hours poring over fabrics and fashion plates, eventually selecting designs that they were confident would make the most of their attractions at the coming ball. More visits to Halifax were arranged, but by mid-December the ladies could at last look forward to the ball, confident in the knowledge that their dress would do them no disservice. When the gowns were finally delivered a few days before Christmas, Mr Worsthorne was required to admire the ladies' finery. The robes were unpacked in the morning-room and Verity dragged Luke from the estate office to view their purchases. She took his arm and led him into the morning-room where the floor was littered with silver tissue.

'Come, Cousin, your estate duties can wait while you see the magnificent gown Madam Juliet has made up for your mama!'

Mrs Worsthorne held up the gown for his inspection.

'There,' cried Verity, 'Is that not wonderful? Your mama will look as fine as fivepence in her gown, will she not?'

Luke smiled. 'And you, Cousin — what will you be wearing?'

Verity swooped upon another large box lying on the sofa and pulled out a shimmering creation in green and gold, sending another cloud of tissue paper drifting to the floor.

'There, Luke,' said Margaret, carefully folding away her own gown, 'will you not be proud to escort two such well-dressed ladies to Newlands?'

'I — am not sure I shall be going.'

Two pairs of eyes turned towards him and the ladies cried out in unison, 'Luke!'

'But why would you not wish to go?' Verity demanded.

'The estate business has fallen behind, and

I can ill afford the time . . . '

'Fiddle! What is there that cannot wait?' she challenged him. 'You have not given me a chance to prove myself yet, but I will help you, if you will let me. After all I need to learn about the estate if I am to manage it half as well as you. Besides,' she added, 'with so few acquaintances, I need you to engage me for the first two dances, at the very least!'

Luke returned her smile and relaxed a little.

'Well, if it means so much to you — '

'Of course it does, to both of us,' declared his mama. 'And if you really mean to stay away, how comes it you have bought yourself a new coat?'

Luke flushed, then gave a self-conscious laugh.

'Gad, Mama! Can a man have no secrets here?'

'It would seem not,' returned Verity, twinkling. 'Now let us hear no more about you staying away!'

★　★　★

Christmas morning dawned damp and cold, but although the roads were muddy, Mrs Worsthorne ordered the carriage to take them to church. She showed some surprise when she learned her son was to accompany them, but she regarded his caped figure riding beside the carriage with no little satisfaction.

'I think it must be your influence, Verity my love, for Luke seldom comes to worship with me.'

As he handed them out of the coach, Verity glanced up at Luke Worsthorne: his upright bearing commanded respect, and his angular features were not unattractive. She was well aware of the envious glances cast their way by several ladies entering the church, but was she pleased to think that he had escorted them solely to gratify her? Verity could not decide, and she was no nearer an answer when they arrived back at Highclough, where the butler informed them in tones of deep disapproval that they had a visitor.

'Mr Reedley has called to see Miss Shore, ma'am,' he addressed Mrs Worsthorne. 'I have put him in the drawing-room, since that has the best fire . . . '

★   ★   ★

Waiting only to put off her coat, Miss Shore hurried to meet her guest, followed closely by Mrs Worsthorne and her son. Mr Reedley bowed as they entered.

'Miss Shore — madam — sir — pray

forgive the intrusion on this special day.'

'No intrusion, sir. Please, will you not sit down? Has Ditton brought you some refreshment?'

Mr Reedley glanced at the tray laden with decanters and glasses that rested on a side table.

'Thank you, but I require nothing. I am merely carrying out a commission given to me by Mr Bannerman.'

Miss Shore's look of surprise caused the old man's lips to curve into the beginnings of a smile.

Mrs Worsthorne stepped forward.

'Perhaps we should all sit down. Luke, please bring another chair closer to the fire for Mr Reedley.'

'If you don't mind, ma'am, I would prefer to stand,' said the lawyer with quiet dignity. 'I shall be spending another hour or more in the saddle on my return journey.' He fixed his faded gaze upon Miss Shore. 'When Mr Bannerman was last in Halifax, he charged me with the duty of collecting a certain item and delivering it here to you. I understand it is not in the nature of a seasonal gift, but circumstances made it impossible for me to bring it to you earlier.'

'Then I am all the more obliged to you for giving up so much of Christmas Day, sir,' replied Verity warmly.

Mr Reedley inclined his head. 'Perhaps, Miss Shore, you would like to read this note, which Mr Bannerman left with me to be given to you with the package.'

Ignoring the small leather box that Mr Reedley pulled from his pocket, Verity took the letter and opened it.

'"The gems Reedley will be delivering belonged to your grandmother," she read. "They are part of a larger set and, as the links were broken, I have had some of the stones reset into something more suitable for you. The remainder of the stones are in safekeeping. RB" Well! What do you make of that?'

Mrs Worsthorne regarded Verity's heightened colour with some unease. 'How kind of Mr Bannerman. Mr Reedley, perhaps you would open the case?'

'Kind! To take it upon himself — oh!' Verity broke off as she caught sight of the necklace. It was lying on a bed of black velvet, a fine gold chain with five small, richly coloured emeralds suspended like tear-drops. A pair of matching ear-rings nestled beside the chain.

The lawyer's tired eyes crinkled into a smile.

'As Mr Bannerman has written in his letter, these are part of a much bigger set which includes among other things an aigrette and a very heavy bracelet — better suited to a matron, if I may say so, Miss Shore?'

'Y-yes, yes of course.' Verity lifted the necklace carefully from its case and gazed at it.

'It is just the thing to wear with your new gown,' remarked Mrs Worsthorne. 'How clever of Master Rafe.'

The mention of Mr Bannerman reminded Verity of her objections.

'It is still most unfeeling of him to make Mr Reedley ride all this way on Christmas Day!'

'As I explained, Miss Shore, Mr Bannerman knew he would not be able to collect the jewels himself and deliver them to you before the ball.'

'Then he should have sent a servant!'

Mr Reedley looked grave. 'Miss Shore, only in the most exceptional circumstances would I condone entrusting such a delicate task to a hireling. Pray believe me when I say that I was only too willing to undertake this mission.'

Miss Shore realized that her anger was misdirected, and did her best to control her indignation.

'Indeed I am most grateful to you, sir, but I

am also mortified to have taken you away from your hearth on this day! Can we not persuade you to sit with us for a while, perhaps take a little refreshment before your journey back to Halifax?'

The lawyer hesitated, then smiled and lowered his thin frame into a chair.

'Well, if you insist. A glass of your fine Malmsey wine and perhaps a biscuit would be very welcome. I must not over-indulge, however, for my good wife is even now preparing a special dinner for us.' He allowed himself another small smile. 'Goose,' he said simply, his eyes twinkling in anticipation.

Luke filled a glass and handed it to the lawyer. 'Mr Bannerman mentioned that the remaining jewels are in safekeeping. Where would that be, do you know?'

Mr Reedley took a moment to choose a biscuit from the plate held out to him by Mrs Worsthorne before replying.

'When Sir Ambrose took to his bed, he summoned Mr Bannerman and myself to the house to make a new will — you may recall the day: he arranged for the Reverend Haskins and one or two of his oldest acquaintances to be present. At that time he handed over his wife's jewels, with orders that Mr Bannerman and I were to see them safely stored with his bankers in Halifax. You need have no fear that they are in danger of being lost,' Mr Reedley assured them. 'Upon Miss Shore's twenty-first birthday, if Mr Bannerman and I consider that she has complied with the terms of the will and is, in Sir Ambrose's words, a fit and proper person to inherit his property, the jewels will be handed over to her. However,' he continued, observing the question forming on Verity's lips, 'when Mr Bannerman came to me and explained his plan for the emeralds, I thought it a most sensible idea, and had no hesitation in supporting him. I do hope that you, too, approve of it, Miss Shore. However, if you do not like the design, the stones can always be replaced in their original setting, or even in some other design of your own choosing.'

Verity stared at the box lying open in her lap. The emeralds gleamed back at her.

'No,' she said quietly, 'I think they are most exquisitely set.'

'Good, good. Then if you will excuse me, I will be on my way. I wish to be home again before dark.'

'Of course you do,' agreed Mrs Worsthorne, rising from her chair. 'And there is your dinner awaiting you.'

'Ah yes, I think I shall have worked up an appetite by then, don't you?' In quiet good humour, the lawyer departed with Mrs

Worsthorne escorting him to the door. Left alone, Luke moved across the room to sit beside Verity.

'Will you wear them at Rafe's party?'

'What? Oh, yes, I think I shall.'

'The stones are yours by right, Cousin. You have no need to feel under any obligation.'

She laughed. 'I don't! That is, I am certainly obliged to Mr Reedley for his labours . . . '

'But you think Bannerman presumes too much?'

She did not answer him immediately, but closed the box gently and held it between her hands.

'Well, perhaps I was a little hasty.'

'It certainly puts my poor gift in the shade.'

Verity thought of the embroidered gloves he had given her that morning.

'Not at all! Did I not wear them to church? Besides, you said yourself that these jewels are rightfully mine, so I do not consider them a Christmas gift at all, although it was a kind thought.'

He caught one of her hands and held it between his own.

'A kind thought, yes, but it was Reedley who carried out the deed.' He paused. 'A true man does not need others to act for him.'

Verity looked up to find Luke watching her.

For a long moment he held her gaze while the ticking of the clock and the crackling fire were the only sounds to break the stillness, then Mrs Worsthorne bustled back into the room.

'Goodness, what a kind man! To ride all this way and stop for barely twenty minutes. I do hope his dinner will not be spoiled.'

Luke released Verity's hands and turned away, his attention caught by a speck on his velvet sleeve, leaving Verity to return a suitable reply to Mrs Worsthorne.

7

A sudden turn in the weather on Boxing Day brought the clouds down over Highclough, enveloping the house in a dull grey mist so that even the tall gates at the end of the drive could not be seen from the house. Rain and high winds lashed the house, keeping the ladies indoors although Mr Worsthorne wrapped himself in his oiled cape and hat and ventured abroad during the day and occasionally in the evening. Although he did not explain his absences to his mother, she confided to Verity her fears that he spent his evenings in Derringden, at the local inn.

'Of course I cannot condone it,' said that lady, twisting the fringe of her shawl between her anxious fingers, 'but what else is there for a young man to do, so far from the town? My hope is that Luke will make new acquaintances at Master Rafe's party. Young men of his own age and calling.'

★ ★ ★

On the day of Mr Bannerman's party, Verity found herself looking out at the leaden sky with some misgivings. After breakfast she went to the great hall, where the howling of the wind echoed around the lofty rafters and the heavy clouds obscured the light, throwing the gallery and the ceiling above it into gloomy darkness.

'Shall we be able to go, do you think?' she asked Mrs Worsthorne.

'Lord yes. Remember we are to dine with Rafe and his guests, so we shall travel there in daylight. Besides, we will be changing into our finery at Newlands, so even if we had to walk part of the way it is of no consequence. Go and pack your things, Verity, my love. You may be sure that our coachman will not be put off by a little rain.'

So it proved, the only change to their plans being that Mr Worsthorne joined them in the carriage instead of riding. As they assembled in the hall before setting off, Mrs Worsthorne expressed her regret that they had not thought to buy Verity an evening cloak.

Verity looked surprised.

'Dear Megs, it was not to be considered.'

'I have no doubt that Madam Juliet could have found something suitable.'

'No doubt you are right, but I agreed with Mr Bannerman that I would buy a gown, nothing more. And he was so generous in giving me the money for my gloves and dancing pumps, I could not impose upon him further.'

'My dear cousin, he was giving you nothing,' Luke reminded her. 'It is your inheritance, after all.'

She flashed him a mischievous smile. 'Only if I prove myself to be a fit and proper person! Until then I exist on your charity.'

Mrs Worsthorne cried out at that and wanted to say more, but Verity would have none of it.

'I am very well pleased with my purchases,' she declared, 'and this woollen cloak affords me excellent protection from the weather. Besides, it will be cast off as soon as we are indoors, so no one will be the wiser.'

★   ★   ★

Despite Mrs Worsthorne's misgivings, Verity was proved right and their arrival at Newlands was observed only by the servants. It was not until the ladies had changed into their gowns and tidied their hair that they were shown into the salon where the dinner guests were assembled. Luke was already there and Verity thought she had never seen him looking better. His fair hair was brushed until it gleamed, his pale colouring enhanced by the dark velvet coat he wore over a white

94

embroidered waistcoat and black satin knee breeches. She flashed a quick smile at him and was rewarded by a warm, appreciative look in return. Verity was indeed in her best looks, the new green gown falling in soft folds which showed her graceful figure to advantage, while the candlelight accentuated the red highlights in her light brown hair. She moved into the room with Mrs Worsthorne and they were soon approached by their host. Mr Bannerman immediately drew the ladies forward to meet his sister.

'Lady Winter has kindly agreed to act as hostess for me,' he explained. 'Is that not so, Sally?'

Lady Winter, a shapely young matron in a diaphanous gown of yellow silk, rose from a sofa and embraced them with her ready smile.

'Of course, dear brother, and I will continue to do so until I can persuade Cook to leave you and come to me! How do you do, ma'am? Such dirty weather — Sir Robin and I came here before Christmas, but I have to say that such savage weather will not do for me. And this is the heiress.' Without pausing for breath Lady Winter turned to Verity, her eyes alight with laughter. 'Delighted, my dear. Rafe has told me all about you. He would have me believe that he rescued you from drudgery, but I have a notion that it is all a sham. He is not at all chivalrous, you know.'

Verity saw the gleam of laughter in that gentleman's eyes as he met her gaze, but she replied without a tremor, 'I was very grateful that he found me, ma'am.'

'And how do you like living in this wild, desolate country? It is a stipulation of the will, is it not, that you live at Highclough?'

'Until my birthday. After that I am free to live where I choose, I believe.' She cast an enquiring glance at Mr Bannerman, who shrugged.

'Of course.'

Mr Worsthorne stepped forward. 'I think Sir Ambrose was convinced that after spending some time at Highclough Miss Shore would not wish to leave it.'

Lady Winter regarded the young gentleman with interest and looked to Mr Bannerman, who performed the introduction.

Lady Winter's smile grew wider.

'So you live at Highclough too?'

'I do, my lady.'

She clapped her hands. 'Better and better! Rafe, you will have to watch your step, or this young man will cut you out with the heiress!'

Verity blushed, but Mr Bannerman merely smiled.

'Sally, you can be so vulgar. Come, Miss

Shore, let me introduce you to our guests. Most are neighbours, and may already be known to you.'

His calm attention to duty did much to restore Verity's composure. He led her towards a stocky gentleman in a brown bag-wig.

'I believe you know Mr Oldroyd, Miss Shore?'

The gentleman had jumped to his feet, smiling broadly as he made his bow.

'Indeed, indeed! We have met upon several occasions now at Derringden church. How do you do, Miss Shore? My wife — where is she, I wonder? She was saying how glad she was that the weather did not prevent you attending.' His faded blue eyes twinkled merrily. 'I know from experience how bad the top routes can be in winter. However, if Bannerman's plans come off we shall all see an improvement hereabouts!'

'Oh, sir, how is that?' asked Verity.

'It is a project Oldroyd and I have been discussing,' put in Mr Bannerman. 'I shall be glad to explain it all to you, Miss Shore, but not tonight! If you will excuse us, sir, I must take Miss Shore away with me: there are several more guests eager to make her acquaintance.'

'Am I really that much of a novelty, sir, or

were you afraid Mr Oldroyd would tell me too much about your plans?'

He smiled. 'A little of both. My ideas are not yet fully formed, and not ready for discussion. And, of even more importance, it is my pleasant duty to introduce you to your new society!'

Verity was happy to accompany him around the room, nodding and smiling and trying to remember as many names as she could, but when the introductions were complete she was more than ready to accept a glass of champagne and accompany her host to a window seat where they sat in companionable silence for several minutes. At length the gentleman's eyes fell to the emerald necklace.

'So you wore it.'

'Did you not think I would?'

'I wondered if you might think me a trifle high-handed.'

This was so close to the truth that Verity laughed, throwing back her head and allowing him an excellent view of the slender column of her neck as well as the emeralds.

'I *did* think it, but the necklace is so beautiful, and such a perfect match for my gown. How did you know?'

'Nothing simpler. I asked Madam Juliet what you had chosen.'

'It was most thoughtful of you. But — '

He grinned. 'I thought I should not remain in grace for long.'

'I cannot approve of you allowing Mr Reedley to undertake the journey to deliver it to me. The poor man rode all the way from Halifax and back on Christmas Day!'

'Did he? Good for him; I knew he would not let me down.'

'It was ill done of you,' she admonished him.

'What else could I do? I was too busy to spend another day in Halifax, and I needed someone I could trust to deliver it. As a co-trustee living in the town, Reedley was the perfect choice. And, may I add, he was only too happy to oblige.'

'Then I will say nothing more about it, except thank you.'

'What I hadn't realized until now is how well the emeralds match your eyes.'

Verity, in the act of sipping her champagne, choked at these audacious words, but the announcement of dinner put an end to their conversation.

Verity was thankful to find herself sitting beside Luke, for although the other guests were perfectly civil, she could not help noticing that with the exception of their host and Lady Winter and her husband, the rest of the dinner guests were very much older. When she mentioned this fact to Luke he smiled.

'They are the elders of our local gentry, cousin. But not, I think, prospective suitors?' he murmured.

She laughed at him, turning it into a cough when several pairs of eyes flickered in her direction. However, as they made their way to the ballroom an hour or so later, she told him, 'I have not given up hope of finding at least one eligible gentleman here tonight!'

Mr Worsthorne looked down at her.

'Are you never serious?'

'Why yes, often! In fact, I will be serious now! You will recall, Cousin, that you offered to dance with me for the first two dances. Pray tell me that you mean to do so! It is such a long time since I danced, except in the schoolroom, and I am quite terrified! You will have to be very patient with me.'

He took her hand and raised it to his lips.

'I am sure you will manage admirably. Now, I can see that Lady Winter is coming to carry you off for more introductions, so I will leave you.'

Suddenly nervous, Verity clung to his hand. 'You will not forget?'

'Of course not.'

Lady Winter dropped on to a small sofa and gave a loud sigh.

'There! Rafe said I was to introduce you to everyone, and I have done so!'

'You excelled yourself, Sally!' Verity laughed and sank down beside her. The two ladies had very quickly become firm friends and dispensed with formality. 'Unfortunately, I cannot remember even half of the names you told me!'

'I would not expect you to do so, although I am sure you will remember the gentlemen who have claimed dances with you. And I am very glad that Robin has secured a dance with you, since I am sitting out this evening.'

'Oh, are you not dancing tonight?'

Lady Winter shook her head and placed her hands over the front folds of her gown.

'I am increasing, and Robin has forbidden me to exert myself, so I must gain what enjoyment I can from watching you!'

A sudden disturbance by the door attracted their attention.

'Oh, a late arrival,' said Verity. 'Look, Sally, do tell me who they are.'

Lady Winter sat up, straining to see through the crowd.

'It is Mrs Wetherby. She is from one of the

oldest and wealthiest families in the county, and considers it adds to her consequence to arrive last at any party! Her husband is just coming in now; he is a magistrate, you know, and the young lady with her is their daughter, Charlotte.'

'Miss Wetherby is very beautiful.'

'And well aware of it.'

Verity glanced at her companion. 'You do not like her?'

'She has been blessed with a large fortune, a good figure and a handsome face, an irresistible attraction for any man. Even my dear brother is ensnared.'

Verity looked across the room as Mr Bannerman greeted Mrs Wetherby and her daughter. She watched as he lifted the young lady's hand to his lips, and a frown creased her brow as he seemed to hold on to those white fingers a fraction longer than was necessary.

'But surely Mr Bannerman does not need — '

'Oh Rafe is rich enough, but what man can resist the chance to increase his fortune?' declared Lady Winter, laughing. 'Now here is that handsome young relative of yours coming to carry you off for the first dance.'

Mr Worsthorne bowed to the ladies.

'As you say, ma'am. Cousin, we should be

taking our place for the first dance.'

Luke was a graceful dancer and Verity felt again that little thrill to note that her partner was attracting admiring glances.

She said as much to him as they took their places in the set.

'Are you glad now that you bought your new coat?' she added mischievously.

He smiled. 'I am glad only if it finds favour with you, Cousin.'

'Well it does! You look very well in it, and the gold fob on your watch-chain, I have not seen that before — is that new too?'

Mr Worsthorne hesitated. 'Yes. A trinket that caught my eye when I was in Leeds before Christmas.'

The start of the dance put an end to their conversation and Verity gave herself up to the enjoyment of the music, but not before she noted that Mr Bannerman was dancing with Miss Wetherby and Lady Winter's words came back to her: what man could resist the chance to increase his fortune?

8

As the evening wore on Miss Shore found she had no time for reflection: her hand was claimed for the next two dances and after that she was content to sit and watch the proceedings. It was a lively party, where most of the guests were well acquainted and at ease with one another. She noticed Mr Bannerman approaching carrying two glasses of champagne.

'I thought you might be in need of refreshment.'

Her eyes twinkled. 'Thank you. Do I look very hot?'

'Not at all, but I saw you were alone . . . '

'My cousin Luke is dancing, and Sir Robin has persuaded Megs to stand up with him. She was determined not to dance, but I am glad she has changed her mind. She knows so many people here!'

'So will you, too, become acquainted with everyone, in time.'

Verity sipped her champagne. 'Miss Wetherby is very pretty. She is much admired in the county, I think?'

'Yes indeed.' He glanced down at her. 'You yourself have not gone unnoticed tonight: several persons have remarked you.'

'Ah, but I have the charm of novelty, sir. I am unknown, and therefore remarkable. Once the weather improves and they see more of me, their interest will wane.'

'You are right, soon you will be nothing more than the poor little female who lives at Highclough.'

Startled, she raised her eyes to his face, relaxing only when she saw his lips curving into a smile.

'Unchivalrous, sir! How can I contradict you without sounding conceited?'

'You can't. But you can have your revenge by coming down to supper with me now: I will then be obliged to make polite conversation with you for a full half-hour.'

She rose and placed one gloved hand on his arm.

'Your conversation, Mr Bannerman, is *never* polite,' she murmured as he led her towards the supper-room.

★　★　★

They found Mrs Worsthorne and her son already sitting at a table with Lady Winter, but even as Mr Bannerman started to guide

Verity towards them, a soft female voice made him pause.

'Will you not join us, sir?'

Verity looked round. Miss Wetherby was smiling and nodding and after the briefest hesitation Mr Bannerman turned back. Moments later, Verity found herself sitting with Mr and Mrs Wetherby and their daughter. Mr Wetherby greeted them with a genial smile before giving his attention to his supper, but it was immediately obvious to Miss Shore that Mr Bannerman was the object of the ladies' attention. She was in no way put out to realize that they considered her a rather insignificant addition to their party. The lack of attention suited her very well and, while enjoying the excellent supper, she took the opportunity to observe Miss Charlotte Wetherby. She was a handsome young woman, possibly a year or two older than Miss Shore, and where Verity's soft brown hair was caught up in a simple green ribbon, Miss Wetherby's golden curls tumbled from a diamond-studded topknot and danced about her shoulders. Her dress of white satin was deceptively simple and probably cost more than the Highclough ladies had spent on both their gowns.

Mrs Wetherby, a formidable matron in a burgundy gown and turban, both lavishly decorated with garnets, was graciously complimenting Mr Bannerman on the success of the evening and, as her daughter was engaged in echoing these sentiments, Verity had nothing to do but enjoy her meal. She was just laying down her fork when Miss Wetherby addressed her.

'I understand, Miss Shore, that you were a governess.'

'Why yes.' She noted Miss Wetherby's look of condescension and added gently, 'It is an occupation considered fitting for *impoverished* young ladies.'

Miss Wetherby recoiled visibly at this, and her mama gave a thin smile.

'As Mistress of Highclough you will no doubt be thankful *that* episode is in the past, Miss Shore.'

'Well, one hopes so,' replied Verity with deceptive sweetness. 'However, I will only inherit Highclough if I am found to be a fit and proper person, and I believe the trustees are not yet convinced — '

'Miss Shore is very fond of levity,' Mr Bannerman interrupted her, a warning in his glance.

'You must forgive dear Charlotte's curiosity, Miss Shore,' remarked Mrs Wetherby. 'My daughter has never had the need to contemplate such a life.'

'Indeed?' replied Verity. 'She is most fortunate.'

'I think it might be rather entertaining,' Miss Wetherby observed, 'to look after dear little children, and to make them mind one.'

Verity smiled. 'Cast your mind back to your own schooldays, Miss Wetherby. Can you truthfully say that you behaved well for your governess?'

'High spirits are only to be expected,' declared Mrs Wetherby, casting a fond glance at her daughter. 'A *good* governess will have no difficulty with that.'

'Not with the children, perhaps,' muttered Verity. Beneath the table she felt Mr Bannerman's foot press down upon her toes but when she looked up he met her gaze with a bland smile as he said, 'I think you would agree Miss Shore, that you are fortunate to be able to give up that role?'

'*Most* fortunate, sir!'

Mrs Wetherby smiled complacently, unaware of the dangerous sparkle in Verity's eyes. 'My dear Miss Shore, you are far too young to have much experience. When dear Charlotte was in need of a governess I chose a much older female to school her, one unlikely to be distracted from her duties.'

'One unlikely to be seduced by the master,' murmured Verity, wincing as she again felt

108

the pressure of Mr Bannerman's foot while the gentleman smoothly addressed Mrs Wetherby.

'I am informed, ma'am, that Miss Shore was a most proficient teacher. When I tracked her down she had the schooling of two lively children at a house in Cromford — '

'Hah, Cromford you say?' Mr Wetherby jerked awake. 'I thought you went there to look at the new mills, Bannerman?'

'Yes. I was invited to visit there, and I took a young engineer with me — James Marsden. He is staying on to study Arkwright's methods, with a view to implementing them for me here. It was a fortunate coincidence that Miss Shore was living in the area.'

But Mr Wetherby was not interested in Miss Shore.

'Well, sir, will it work, d'you think? Using these infernal machines for spinning?'

'Yes, I think it might.' Mr Bannerman pushed his plate away. 'The machines never stop, you see. The workforce is divided into two shifts, and the lights blaze from the mill throughout the night. Such a mill here would keep every weaver in the area busy.'

'But Arkwright's mills use cotton, I believe.'

'Yes, but there are many practices that would work as well for wool, or worsted.

109

That's what Marsden is to determine.' He leaned forward, warming to his theme. 'At the present time the farmers can only sell their fleeces to the staplers who sort the wool and sell on the yarn for spinning. My plan is to set up our own mill here in the valley, where we can purchase the wool direct, giving the farmers a better price. Once it is spun, the yarn can be put back out to the cottagers for weaving. You know we have the finest wool in England on these hills, and by keeping the industry local I believe we can improve everyone's lot.'

Mr Wetherby looked sceptical.

'But what do you know about spinning, Bannerman? What in fact do you know about wool?'

Rafe Bannerman grinned. 'Very little, but I have every faith in Marsden. He is the son of a local weaver, so he knows the trade. We've the best wool in the country here, Wetherby, and you know it. Long-staple wool, perfect for worsteds. I want to make the most of that, and if I can improve the lot of my tenants and the small-holders on the hills, so much the better. Besides, these new methods are coming, whether we like 'em or not, and if we don't move now the work will go to Halifax and Bradford and our local people will suffer.'

Mr Wetherby shook his head. 'Bannerman, I don't hold with these new ideas, breaking up the old order. It does no good, only look at the trouble it's caused in France.'

'But surely, Mr Wetherby, that was precisely because they would not change from the old order,' put in Verity. She found all eyes turned upon her and coloured. 'That is, there was no attempt in France to improve the lot of the poor. I believe everyone is entitled to earn a living.'

'Well done, Miss Shore,' murmured Mr Bannerman, his eyes glinting.

'By Gad, miss, you are very young to be expressing yourself so!' declared Mr Wetherby, eyeing her uncertainly.

Miss Wetherby began to fidget. 'Well, I for one find the subject most tedious! Mr Bannerman, pray take me back to the ballroom, for I am sure it is time for the dancing to begin again!'

Taking the hint, Miss Shore rose smoothly to her feet.

'I believe you are right, Miss Wetherby. I can see my cousin looking for me, so I shall take my leave of you.'

She sketched a slight curtsy to the party and made her way across to Mrs Worsthorne, who was preparing to leave the room with Lady Winter.

'My love, I have been watching you all through supper! How animated you all looked! How do you like Miss Wetherby? Would it not be wonderful if you two were to become close friends?'

'Wonderful indeed, Megs. I fear she is too well bred for my taste.'

'I do not understand you.'

Verity's green eyes sparkled with anger. 'The lady is too full of her own importance. I do not think she felt at ease conversing with a *mere governess!* In fact, I wanted nothing better than to shock her out of her complacence.' Her lips twitched. 'Fortunately Mr Bannerman was on hand to remind me of my manners.'

'Rafe playing propriety, I cannot believe it!' Lady Winter clapped her hands. 'Oh bravo, Verity! I made sure you would not like her — and my poor brother, is he besotted then?'

Verity spread her hands.

'He may well be. Miss Wetherby and her mama paid him every attention, and agreed with every word he uttered!'

Lady Winter gave a little crow of laughter.

'Poor Rafe, he will be bored to death! Come, let us go back to the ballroom and watch the rest of this merry farce!'

★   ★   ★

'Well, Miss Shore, are you enjoying yourself?'

Verity looked round to find her host standing beside her.

'Very much so, Mr Bannerman! My experience of parties is limited, but this is so lively, everyone in such good spirits — you are to be congratulated, sir.'

'For what? I have done very little, merely brought in the musicians and laid on good food and wine. Where is the skill in that?'

'I cannot say, but there must be something.'

'The people perhaps? Do you think I have a gift for throwing together those with similar minds — like yourself and Miss Wetherby, for instance?'

Verity smiled but shook her head. 'I was very rag-mannered, it was bad of me. But it is not only my conscience that is nagging me — my poor toes are still hurting!'

He grinned at her. 'Yes, I'm sorry about that, but I could see you had lost your temper and were in danger of uttering something you would later regret.'

'So uncivil of me,' she retorted, 'when I feel sure the Wetherbys were trying to put me at my ease.'

'Trying to put you in your place would be more the case! You know that and so do I. Can't have a little upstart governess coming

113

into the area and taking the shine out of all the local beauties!'

Verity gave a little crow of laughter.

'I am sure you are wrong there! Miss Wetherby must be ignorant of her own considerable charms if she is afraid of that!'

'Oh Miss Wetherby is well aware of her, ah, charms, as you put it, but since she does not have your generosity of spirit she cannot bear to admit to any other woman's attractions.'

'Is — is that a compliment, sir?' Verity asked him, startled.

'Possibly.' He held out his hand to her. 'Come and dance with me.'

'Thank you. And to demonstrate my *generosity of spirit*, I will do my best to be agreeable, sir, and not to contradict you.'

'I beg your pardon?'

'Is that not what pleases a gentleman, to be fawned upon and flattered?'

'Not this gentleman!'

'I confess I should find it difficult to concur with everything you say.'

His eyes glinted. 'I knew I could depend upon you to add a little spice to the evening.'

'Well, I hope I don't add too much — I am a little out of practice at country dances.'

'Don't worry, I was watching you earlier — you danced beautifully.'

The compliment was uttered in a matter-of-fact tone but Verity flushed, gratified as they took their places in the set. She enjoyed dancing with Mr Bannerman, for he was a graceful dancer, his clasp on her hand was reassuring as he led her through the movements. She knew a moment's regret when the music ended and he led her off the floor.

'Let me take you to my sister,' he said. 'My duty as a host precludes my dancing with you again.'

'Your tone does not suggest you regret the fact, sir.'

'No, my feet need time to recover.'

Verity gasped. 'How dare you! You know I trod on you but once.'

His dark eyes glinted down at her. 'Only because I took care to keep well away from you, I thought after my — er — gentle remonstrance with you at supper you might be out for revenge.'

'It would be no more than you deserve, Mr Bannerman!'

'Hush now, or Sally will hear you, and think you no better than a fishwife to be scolding so.'

She choked, aware of the novel sensation of wanting to laugh at a gentleman and murder him at the same time.

He led her up to Lady Winter, then with a brief word, he was gone, and Verity stood beside her hostess, watching his departing form. Lady Winter smiled at her.

'Well my dear, you have such a glow about you I need not ask if you are happy! Would you like me to find you another dancing partner? It is the last chance, I think, for people are beginning to depart.'

But Verity found she did not want to dance again. Excusing herself, she made her way around the edge of the ballroom, looking for a secluded corner where she could be alone with her thoughts.

'Cousin — are you looking for Mama?' Mr Worsthorne came up to her.

'No, that is, does she look for me?'

'Not at all.' He grinned. 'She is catching up on several weeks' gossip.'

'Good. I was looking for somewhere quiet . . . '

He took her arm. 'I know the house a little — come with me.' He led her out of the ballroom and across the hall to a set of double doors that opened into the library. The candles had burned down in their sockets, but several were still alight, giving the room a cosy glow, and a cheerful fire crackled in the hearth.

'Will this suit you?'

'Perfectly.'

She allowed him to lead her to a sofa placed before the fire. She sank down, gazing into the flames and not seeming to notice that he was still holding her hand.

'You are fatigued,' he observed. 'We are not used to such late hours at Highclough.'

'Indeed not, although I have enjoyed it immensely.'

'We could dance at Highclough, there is the ballroom, you know, Cousin.' His free hand rested along the back of the sofa, and she felt his fingers playing with the ringlets on the nape of her neck. 'Verity, you have been at Highclough for only two months, but already I feel I know you very well.'

'Luke, please.' Something in his tone alarmed her. He put his fingers to her lips.

'No, let me finish. I know it's too soon, but I've grown to care for you, Verity, and I think you are not indifferent to me.'

'Not indifferent, but — ' She paused, noting the earnest look in his eyes. 'Luke, you are very sweet, and I *do* care for you, but in a brotherly sort of way.'

'That could change.'

She shook her head, resolutely meeting his gaze.

'No, Luke.' She smiled and gently put one hand to his cheek. 'It would be very wrong of me to give you hope where none exists. You and Megs are very dear to me, Cousin, I should hate to lose you now. Pray tell me we may still be friends?'

She saw him frown, as if struggling with his emotions, before he gave a slight nod. He reached up and caught her hand, pulling it round to press a kiss into its palm.

'Aye. As you wish, Cousin.'

He spoke so wistfully that she was obliged to brush away a tear.

'I am sorry if I intrude.'

At the sound of Rafe Bannerman's harsh voice they sprang apart. Verity rose hastily from the sofa, aware of the blush spreading over her cheeks.

'Mrs Worsthorne is wishing to retire, and is looking for you both.'

Luke got to his feet in a leisurely style. 'Thank you. We will go to her immediately.'

Following Mr Worsthorne to the door, Verity glanced up at Mr Bannerman as she passed and saw such searing anger and accusation in his eyes that her cheeks flamed. She shrank away from him, as if afraid he might strike out at her and hurried back to the ballroom, aware that her enjoyment of the evening was at an end.

★　★　★

By the morning, Miss Shore's naturally sunny temperament had reasserted itself. If Mr Bannerman had misconstrued the nature of her *tête-à-tête* with Luke Worsthorne she thought it would be a simple matter to explain. Unfortunately, she had no opportunity to do so. Apart from a cold nod in greeting as she entered the breakfast-room, Mr Bannerman made no effort to speak to her. At their departure, he bade them all a polite but brief farewell and went off to his book-room, leaving Lady Winter to see them off.

'Goodbye, Verity my dear.' Lady Winter hugged her. 'I promise I shall visit you very soon. Robin returns home at the end of the week, but I will remain here for some weeks yet, so we shall have time to become great friends.'

'Oh I do hope so,' murmured Verity, returning her embrace. 'I have so much enjoyed your company.'

★　★　★

Highclough seemed very empty after the crowded bustle of Newlands, but Verity was optimistic that she would soon settle into its domestic routine. Luke was surly and quiet at first, and Verity forced herself to refer to their conversation at Newlands. She had asked if she might ride out with him, and waited until they were a safe distance from the house before broaching the subject.

'Luke, what we said, at Newlands.' She sensed his tension and hurried on, 'I like you too well to lie to you, Cousin. I have grown so fond of you, and I do so want us to be friends.'

He turned toward her, frowning. She held out her hand.

'Come, Cousin,' she coaxed him. 'You have not known me long enough to have developed a lasting passion! Pray take my hand, and cry friends with me!'

After a brief hesitation he shrugged and grasped her fingers.

'Very well, Cousin.'

'There! Now we can be comfortable again! I dislike being at odds with anyone, and I really do value your friendship, Luke.'

He nodded, his face set, and she realized that he had conceded as much as he was going to do for one day, and she spent the rest of the ride chatting away to him, trying to dispel the last remnants of his stony resistance.

After that she made a point of riding out with Luke whenever the weather and his duties permitted, getting to know the tenants and clothiers who lived in the small farmsteads dotted over the slopes. In the face of such a determined assault Mr Worsthorne's reserve gradually dwindled and Verity felt they had gone a long way towards restoring harmony.

9

At the end of January the weather worsened, the temperature dropped and two weeks of hard frosts followed. Icy winds scoured the hills and a scattering of snow dusted the high moors. A message from Newlands brought word from Lady Winter that her husband and her brother had forbidden her to travel in such conditions, so with no prospect of visitors, the Highclough ladies busied themselves indoors. Passing through the hall one day, Verity looked out of the window and was intrigued to see several of the house servants making their way to the pond. They were armed with various long-handled nets and saws. She stopped to watch.

'Cousin? Is anything amiss?' Mr Worsthorne called down to her from the gallery.

'What are they doing at the lake?'

Luke came to stand beside her.

'They are collecting ice. We have a store built into the garden, behind the west wing. They will take the ice there, and add more to it through the winter, if the weather remains cold. It can then be used during the summer, for sorbets, among other things.'

Verity laughed. 'How delightful!'

'Yes. The winters here can be something savage, so it's comforting to think we receive some benefit, however frivolous!' He moved away. 'Now, Cousin, you wanted to see the rent books?'

★ ★ ★

The bitter winter weather continued, the temperature rising only enough to bring another fall of snow. Verity had just resigned herself to another week confined indoors when Rafe Bannerman came trotting along the drive on his black hunter. Clutching her shawl around her, Verity hurried out to meet him.

'Mr Bannerman! Welcome, sir, I am so glad to see you!'

He had been frowning, but her words made him smile.

'Well that is prettily said, at all events,' he remarked, dismounting. 'Are you quite well, Miss Shore?'

'Exceedingly bored with my own company! Luke is working out of doors and Megs is busy writing letters, so I am left to amuse myself, which I am finding very tedious this morning. Come into the house. Brigg will take your horse to the stables.' She beckoned to the groom, who was hovering in the shadow of the building. 'We have been making a few changes. I discovered a harpsichord which we have moved into the morning-room — it was in the ballroom, which is far too cold and never used.' She took Mr Bannerman's arm and led him indoors. 'We have a fire kindled in the morning-room every day, you see, and Megs and I spend most evenings in there if we are alone, which is usually the case.'

He was quick to detect the wistful note in her voice.

'You wish for more company?'

'No, no — well, that is, not often. Although it can be a little quiet here.' She cast a quick glance up at him through her lashes. 'I've no doubt that you are constantly entertaining visitors ... Mr and Mrs Wetherby, for instance?'

The disturbing twinkle appeared in his eyes and she flushed.

'You will be pleased to know that I have not seen Mr and Mrs Wetherby — or their daughter — since the New Year party.'

'Pleased, sir?' she said airily. 'Wh-why on earth should it matter to me if you have seen the Wetherbys?'

'Oh? Was not that the reason for you mentioning them?' he responded, in the same

124

light tone. 'Sally seemed to think you might be pleased to know that Miss Wetherby is no longer . . . what was her phrase? Throwing her cap at me. My ideas are too modern to suit her parents. My company embarrasses them.'

Verity choked, but her companion did not appear to notice.

'And if we are talking of company, Miss Shore, I would have thought Worsthorne would have been with you most evenings.'

'No. That is, he — he has business that often keeps him in Halifax, and if he is at Highclough he likes to meet with friends in Derringden of an evening. Please do not think I blame him — he is young, after all, to be tied to Highclough day and night.'

'The same might be said of you, madam.'

'My case is different, sir. As a governess I am used to keeping my own company.'

'If Worsthorne has time on his hands, I wonder he does not look to his Sowerby estates. I understand he has not been near them for months.' He saw her anxious look and shook his head. 'Forgive me, I did not come here to criticize. Tell me instead how you fill your days; are you at daggers drawn with Mrs Worsthorne?'

'Of course not! We rub along very well, for Megs has the sunniest nature imaginable.'

'While you, of course, are for ever at odds with the world.'

She laughed. 'Only with you, sir, and I lay the blame for much of that squarely at your door! But to be serious — with music, and books, and sometimes backgammon as well as keeping household, we occupy ourselves very well. When the weather improves I shall make a start on restoring the shrubbery within the walled garden. I intend to make a sketch of the garden as it is now, as soon as it is warm enough to sit outside.'

'An admirable idea. Do you require drawing materials — can I fetch you anything from Halifax?'

'Thank you, but I gave Luke a list of my needs and he fetched everything last week. I also ride out with him when I can, so that I am gradually becoming familiar with the estate.'

'Good. And now you have mentioned riding — my sister has asked if you would care to have her mare for the next few months? She brought the horse with her to Newlands, but Sir Robin does not think it wise for her to ride in her present state.'

'And she would trust me with her mare?'

'I have told her how well you ride.'

'Th-thank you, but, I could not — '

'The creature might as well be of use here

as eating her head off in my stables, you know.'

'Well, in that case I cannot refuse, when you put it so elegantly, sir! Please thank Lady Winter for me, I shall accept her generous offer.'

'You may thank her yourself, for she intends to visit you in a day or two, and she will bring the mare with her.'

★ ★ ★

With this treat to look forward to, Verity found her spirits rising. Even the weather improved and a few days later she put on her warmest gown, wrapped herself in her cloak and took her sketch pad outside. The shrubbery was contained within a walled enclosure at the eastern end of the main building. Verity sat down on the stone bench that had been placed against the house wall. It was ideally suited to take advantage of the morning sun, while the high walls kept off any chilly breeze. Verity smiled as she felt the February sun warm her cheeks, then she turned her attention to sketching the overgrown shrubbery. She was making good progress when she heard the sound of carriage wheels on the drive. Assuming it was the servants returning with fresh supplies she continued with her drawing, until she heard Lady Winter's cheerful voice calling to her.

'Sally!' She jumped up and ran forward as Lady Winter appeared at the stone archway, her hands tucked inside a frivolous swansdown muff. Verity's smile wavered as she saw the look of horror on Lady Winter's face, but before she could speak there was a loud crash behind her. Verity swung round. The bench where she had been sitting a moment earlier was now smashed into little pieces.

★   ★   ★

Verity stared. A large block of stone lay amongst the remains of the bench. Clutching tightly at her sketch-pad to stop her hands from trembling, she looked towards the roof. Two square chimney stacks rose toward the sky and there was a large gap in the side of one of the stacks.

'Oh thank God you were not hurt. I saw the stone falling but was too shaken to say a word!'

Lady Winter's quavering voice brought Verity to her senses. She hurried towards her.

'Poor Sally, I am so sorry — we will go indoors immediately and find you a restorative. What a shock for you.'

'Even more of a shock for you!' replied my

lady with a shaky laugh. 'By all means let us go in — Rafe rode over with me. We could not find your groom so he took the horses to the stable while I came to find you.' She leaned on Verity's proffered arm and walked with her to the front door, where Verity sent a footman scurrying off to fetch brandy.

The two ladies went into the morning-room, where they found Mr Bannerman standing beside the fire, conversing with Mrs Worsthorne.

At the sight of Lady Winter's pale face Megs exclaimed, 'Oh my heavens — Lady Winter!'

Mr Bannerman crossed the room in two strides and put his arm about his sister.

'Sally, what is it, what is the matter?'

'It is nothing — I shall be well again in an instant, but pray look after Verity — sit down, child, you look so pale I fear you will faint.'

Verity managed a wan smile. 'I never faint, but I will sit down.'

'What happened?' demanded Mr Bannerman.

'A s-stone fell from the roof, into the shrubbery.' Verity tried to speak calmly. 'It has s-smashed the bench beyond repair, I'm afraid.'

'Such a fortunate escape!' declared Lady

129

Winter. 'Poor Verity was sitting on that very bench a moment earlier! Thank goodness that you got up when you heard me calling you, or heaven knows — '

Mrs Worsthorne threw up her hands, her plump cheeks quite white.

'Merciful heavens.'

'Megs, I am not hurt,' Verity tried to reassure her. 'My concern is for Lady Winter — ah, here is Ditton with the brandy. Megs, will you please take charge, I fear my limbs are trembling too much for me to stand up.' She smiled, and fought back a ridiculous urge to cry.

'Brigg told me there had been an accident.' Mr Worsthorne came striding in. 'Cousin, are you hurt?'

'No, by the most fortunate chance!' declared his mama. 'Verity has narrowly escaped death!'

Verity shook her head. The brandy had done much to restore her.

'No, no, Cousin. It is not as bad as all that. A stone fell from the roof — from the chimney in fact. It has destroyed the bench in the shrubbery.'

'But only think, Luke!' declared Mrs Worsthorne. 'Poor Verity had been sitting on that very bench only seconds earlier, and Lady Winter saw the stone fall!'

Mr Worsthorne frowned. 'You saw it, ma'am?'

Lady Winter shook her head. 'Only something dropping behind Verity, but it was all so sudden. Rafe and I rode over — I am leaving my hack here for Verity to use, you see. We had arranged for the carriage to follow on and take me back. Ditton told me Verity was sketching in the shrubbery so I thought I would find her while Rafe saw to the horses. Thank goodness I was not a moment later.'

'A dreadful experience, for both of you,' said Luke.

'Well, I am much recovered now.' Lady Winter handed her empty glass to her brother. 'But, Verity my dear, you are much too pale, perhaps you should lie down?'

Miss Shore shook her head.

'No, no. I promise I shall not fret over what might have been. I shall do very well, if I sit quietly for a little longer.'

'Well, well, what excitement!' Mrs Worsthorne sank down on to a sofa, mopping her brow with a lacy handkerchief. 'Luke, you must go up on to the roof immediately and make sure no more stones are loose.'

'Yes, please do.' Verity tried to smile. 'I have no wish for any more such accidents. I am sure Megs would not like to inherit

Highclough in such a way.'

Mr Bannerman raised his brows.

'Inherit Highclough?'

'Well, yes.' Verity looked at him. 'If I die, surely Megs would inherit everything, as Sir Ambrose's nearest relation?'

'Nearly everything,' said Mr Bannerman. 'But by the terms of the will, if *you* do not inherit Highclough, Miss Shore, it comes to me.'

10

There was an uncomfortable silence in the room.

'Forgive me,' stammered Verity, 'I assumed . . .'

'A very natural assumption,' Mr Bannerman said. He looked across at Mr Worsthorne, who was pouring brandy into a glass.

'I take it you knew of this, Luke?'

'As a matter of fact, no. I did not attend the reading of the will — I was laid up with a sprained ankle at the time, if you remember.' He swore softly as the spirit spilled over the edge of the glass.

'I am sorry, then, if the news is unwelcome.' Mr Bannerman spoke quietly, his eyes fixed on the younger man.

Luke turned. 'Unwelcome? Why should it be?'

The challenge hung in the air. Verity looked at the two men, a slight frown creasing her brow. Mrs Worsthorne flapped her hands.

'No doubt I should have informed you, Luke, had I thought of it, but if truth be told it seemed of little import, for Mr Reedley and Master Rafe had no doubt they would find

Charles's child, and then there was your own legacy, the property at Sowerby — that seemed so generous of Sir Ambrose . . . '

Luke shrugged. 'Pray do not distress yourself, Mama, it is of little matter, after all.'

Despite his nonchalant tone, Verity was aware of the tension crackling in the room. At that moment the butler entered and Lady Winter rose unsteadily to her feet.

'Here is Ditton come to tell us my carriage is here. It will be dark within the hour, Rafe. We must go . . . '

The spell was broken: goodbyes were said, and Verity accompanied the lady outside.

'I hope there will be no lasting damage from this afternoon, Sally,' she murmured, as Mr Bannerman helped his sister into the carriage and leaned in to tuck a warm rug over her knees.

Lady Winter smiled. 'Of course not! I was merely a little shaken. It is *you* we should be cosseting! I hope the incident has not given you a distaste for Highclough.'

'Not at all, but I shall have the building checked thoroughly before I venture out of doors again!'

Mr Bannerman turned towards her, smiling.

'A sensible precaution. Goodbye, Miss

Shore.' He took her hand. 'I shall be busy with my own estates for the next few weeks, but I will call when I can.'

Lady Winter leaned forward. 'I hope you like my mare, I call her Delphi. She has the sweetest nature. And I shall not be riding again until after my confinement in April.'

'I think I shall love her!' laughed Verity. 'Thank you.'

With a final nod, Mr Bannerman stepped up into the carriage and the coach pulled away, leaving Verity to hurry indoors, where she found Mrs Worsthorne in a state of agitation. It took Verity some time to assure that good lady that she had taken no hurt from the falling stone, and only after Luke had promised to go up to the roof himself and check the masonry could Mrs Worsthorne be easy.

★　★　★

A spell of bright days followed, although the sharp frosts at night kept a coating of snow on the higher moors. Verity was eager to try out her new mount, and it was not long before she persuaded Luke to ride out with her. The mare was very different from Mrs Worsthorne's ageing hack and Verity returned exhilarated by her excursion. Her cheeks were still glowing from the exercise when she sat down to dinner, causing Mrs Worsthorne to comment.

'Well I *did* enjoy myself, Megs,' she responded, smiling. 'Luke was a little anxious because the mare was so fresh, but she is beautifully mannered, and we kept a most decorous pace!'

Luke grinned across the table at her.

'Much to your annoyance, Cousin! But you are not yet familiar with the country; the rocky ground and hidden peat bogs make it very easy to take a tumble.'

'That did not prevent you from racing me to Bridestones,' she threw at him, eyes twinkling.

'Only because you would have gone ahead on your own, if I had not!'

'Children, children, pray do not bicker at the dinner-table!' cried Mrs Worsthorne, laughing.

'Very well, Mama, but I would have you support me in one thing: my cousin is determined to ride out alone.'

'And why should I not?' returned Verity. 'Megs dislikes riding, and you are very often busy with your business — it is nonsensical for me to drag either one of you with me.'

'I know it seems that way, Cousin, but the moors can be treacherous. If you must go out, promise me that you will take Brigg with you.'

Verity hesitated. She did not like the taciturn groom with his weasel face and eyes that would never meet her own.

'Please, Cousin,' Luke spoke quietly. 'I would not have you riding out over the moors alone.'

'Very well. To please you.' She smiled at him. 'I will take him with me when I ride over to Newlands tomorrow!'

★　★　★

The morning dawned fine and sunny, but when Verity rode out at noon the ground was still hard in the shadows where the sun could not reach. Lady Winter's mare danced and sidled playfully as Verity trotted out of the stable yard with the groom at a respectful distance behind her. As they climbed from the farmland on to the moors the wind picked up and Verity pushed Delphi into a canter. As they reached the Bridestones she saw that the enclosure was filled with pack-ponies. At the entrance, sprawled between the two upright stones was a long-limbed individual in a brown suit. He was wearing a broad-brimmed hat, which he raised as she approached, bidding her good-day in a deep rich drawl. Verity nodded, noting the wedge of ham pie and flagon of ale on the ground beside him. She brought her mare to a halt.

'Which way do you go?'

The man touched his hat again.

'To Derringden, ma'am, then on to Halifax in the morning.'

'And what do you carry?'

'Gewgaws for the ladies.' He winked at her. 'Lace and ribbons, combs and love-knots, pinchbeck rings and pewter snuff-boxes for the lads.'

'And does your route take you past Highclough?'

'Aye,' he said slowly. 'It could do.'

'If you call there you may have use of the stables for the night, if you care to sleep in the hayloft.' Her eyes gleamed. 'I have a mind to purchase some ribbons.'

'Much obliged to you, ma'am.' The man touched his hat as Verity rode away.

'Master won't be none too pleased at that,' muttered Brigg, as he turned his horse to follow her.

'Oh?'

'He don't hold with the packmen coming through.'

'I understood Sir Ambrose always allowed them to stay.'

'Aye, he did, but Master Luke put a stop to it when the old master was ill. There's shelter enough in the valley for them as needs it.'

Verity halted. She looked at the groom, then turned her mare back towards the packman, who had finished his pie and was packing away the remains of his meal.

'If I am not back when you reach Highclough,' she said, 'tell them Miss Shore sent you.'

'Aye, ma'am. That I will.' The old man looked up at her, a twinkle in his black eyes. 'You be the new Highclough lady then?'

'Yes,' she said. 'I am the Highclough lady.'

* * *

Riding into the stable yard at Newlands a short time later, she found Mr Bannerman coming out of one of the stalls. He was dressed as befitted a country gentleman in a brown coat and tight-fitting buckskins, but there was no speck of mud on his gleaming top boots.

'Good morning, sir. Are you about to go out riding?'

'No. Sally was bored and had a fancy to try a little archery and insisted I set up the targets. Then the packman arrived and she found herself obliged to inspect his latest collection of trinkets, so I have been packing everything away again.' As she halted the mare he stepped forward to lift her down from the saddle. 'So you are finding your way around now. Do you like the mare?'

'Very much indeed! I am so grateful to your sister for allowing me to use her!'

'Then you may tell her so yourself, for she is in the morning-room.'

'But dare I brave your housekeeper and enter in all my dirt?'

'I will make sure you wipe your boots before you enter, and find you a joint-stool to sit upon, so that you do not sully the covers.'

She laughed. 'How ungallant of you! You deserve that I should turn about and leave immediately.'

'No, don't do that, Sally would be most disappointed.' His eyes turned towards Brigg, who was leading the horses into the stable.

'My cousin insists that I do not ride alone,' explained Verity, as she accompanied him to the house.

'Very wise. The moors can be treacherous. Come inside: Sally will be delighted to display her purchases to a more appreciative audience!'

'This packman — a tall, thin man in brown homespun? I have seen him at Bridestones.'

'That will be the one.'

'I have asked him to call at Highclough — I have also said he may stay the night, although I think my cousin may disapprove.'

'You need not worry, old Jason is safe enough.' He led her into the morning-room, where Lady Winter was reclining on a day-bed. 'Don't get up, Sally, but you have a visitor. Now if you will excuse me, I will go and change, and leave you ladies to talk of fashion and furbelows!'

Left alone, the two ladies enjoyed a comfortable hour, with Mr Bannerman joining them again when the tea tray was brought in.

'I thought you had deserted us, Brother.' Lady Winter moved towards the fire and began the ritual of making tea.

'I had letters to write. Besides, I have no interest in fashion.'

'Considerate of you, then, to stay away,' remarked Verity.

The gentleman's lips twitched. 'I thought so.'

Another hour slipped by in lively conversation before the fading light reminded Verity that the short March day was drawing to a close.

She took her leave of Lady Winter and allowed Mr Bannerman to escort her back to the stables.

'This clear sky means another sharp frost,' said the gentleman, throwing her up into the saddle. 'Take care on the lanes.'

'I will. Will you visit Highclough soon, sir?'

'If the weather remains good I shall bring Sally over again before her husband returns to fetch her home next week.'

'I shall look forward to it.' Verity waited for Brigg to scramble into the saddle then flashed a final smile at her host.

'Goodbye, sir.'

'Goodbye, Miss Shore. The light will hold until you get home, but don't dawdle!'

★　★　★

The sun was already gone from the valley, but as the riders moved up on to the moors it could still be seen low on the horizon, an angry red ball that set fire to the hills and threw the rocky outcrops into strong relief. As they rode clear of the highest enclosures, Verity heard the groom calling out to her. She reined in.

'My horse is lame, miss.' Brigg jumped down and picked up one of the animal's feet, inspecting it closely. 'I shall have to walk her the rest of the way, but you should go on — 'tis too cold now for you to wait for me. Go ahead, miss, if you please, and tell 'em I'll be coming in later.'

Verity nodded. An icy wind had sprung up and she was eager to be moving.

'I'll send someone out with a lantern to meet you,' she said, then with a final nod at the groom she set off at a smart pace across the moors.

★ ★ ★

The sun dipped beyond the hills and Verity braced herself against the icy wind that cut through her riding habit. She had gone about half a mile when the mare snorted, throwing up her head.

'Whoa there.' Verity looked around, but could see nothing unusual around her. 'Easy, girl, there's nothing there.'

She leaned forward to pat the smooth neck, but as she did so the mare snorted again and leapt forward, breaking into a canter along the path. Verity tried in vain to check her but the horse had the bit firmly between her teeth. She began to buck and sidle, trying to unseat Verity, and when that did not work Delphi set off at a gallop, careering madly over the uneven ground. Verity's attempts to halt the mare were futile, the animal plunged onwards, leaving the path towards High-clough for a grassy lane that swept down from the moors towards a steep, shadowed valley. Verity hung on grimly, concentrating on staying in the saddle until the animal grew tired. The path led them downwards, winding perilously around the edge of the steep valley-side. Verity was beginning to wonder if she would be able to find her way back in the growing darkness when the mare suddenly sat back on her haunches and stopped, sending the rider flying over her head and into the valley below.

★　★　★

Mrs Worsthorne stood by the window in the great hall, peering out into the darkness. Her round face was creased with anxiety.

'Perhaps she has stayed to dine with Rafe and his sister,' suggested Luke.

'No, no, for surely she would have sent word.'

'Mama, do not worry. She has Brigg with her. Mayhap Verity delayed too long and the fading light would surely slow the return journey. Let me light the candles in here.'

'No.' She waved him away. 'I want to look out for her.'

Luke sighed and put his arm about his mama.

'It is a clear night: they will be even now be

making their way along the lanes, you will see. Set dinner back an hour, and if my cousin has not appeared by then I will send a couple of men out to look for her.'

'Yes, Luke, thank you. That would help.' Mrs Worsthorne turned again to the window. The clear sky had darkened to a deep blue, with the occasional star twinkling.

She shivered, pulling her shawl closer about her shoulders as she sank down on to the cushioned window-seat. 'Pray send a message to Cook, love. And have them build up the fire. The poor child will be chilled to the bone when she comes in.'

Left alone with her thoughts, Mrs Worsthorne peered out anxiously into the darkness. Perhaps Luke was right and Verity had accepted an invitation to dine at Newlands: Sally Winter might even have persuaded her to remain overnight, and a servant would be even now bringing a message to Highclough. She glanced up at the starry night. The clear sky would afford some light to travellers, even though it would bring another sharp frost. Mrs Worsthorne maintained her vigil at the window until the clock chimed another hour. She was about to go in search of Luke and insist that he send out a search-party when she spotted a dark shadow on the drive. With a small cry of relief she leaned towards the glass, expecting to see two riders. Instead she could make out only the shape of one horse being led up to the house by Brigg. Mrs Worsthorne flew to the front door but as she stepped outside she saw that Luke was there before her.

'What is it!' she demanded. 'Where is Miss Shore?'

'Brigg doesn't know, Mama. His horse went lame and he had to walk back, so Cousin Verity rode on ahead.'

'Oh dear heaven!' cried Mrs Worsthorne, throwing up her hands.

'Go inside, Mama. I will set out immediately with some of the servants to look for her.' He turned to his groom. 'Take your horse to the stable, then you and the rest of the stable lads join me here with as many lanterns as you can muster. Quickly!'

Luke gently guided his mother inside. 'Wait for us here, Mama, and never fear: we shall find her.'

★ ★ ★

Verity opened her eyes and found herself staring up at smoke-blackened rafters. She moved her head and a groan escaped her as a pain shot across her eyes. Immediately a figure was bending over her. A hushed female voice spoke to her.

'Does it hurt, lass? Take some of this. No, no, don't fret, miss. 'Tis only valerian root to help you rest until the doctor can get here.'

Verity swallowed the liquid, closing her eyes gratefully as the woman placed a cool damp cloth on her burning temples. She heard voices murmuring somewhere in the room but could not understand the words, and soon she found herself drifting into unconsciousness.

★ ★ ★

When she awoke again it was daylight and the rosy glow of the rising sun was shining across her bed. Cautiously she moved her head. The pain had eased a little and she was able to take note of her surroundings. She was in a small, low room with a large fireplace at one end, where a woman was spinning busily before a cheerful blaze. The smell of wood smoke was mixed with a faint odour of the stables but Verity was so thankful to be lying down this did not worry her. Her bed was a wooden settle with a thin mattress that did little to support Verity's aching limbs. To her tender senses the noises of the house were magnified, the rhythmic hum of the spinning wheel, the black kettle singing merrily above the crackling of the fire and a steady thump, thump from the room above.

The woman stopped her spinning.

'Eh lass, art thou awake? I've been waiting for 'ee to open your eyes. I'll put the kettle on. The doctor'll be 'ere any time now, and I 'spect he'd appreciate a hot drink.'

'Where am I?' Verity's throat was very dry and the words were little more than a whisper.

'Lie still, lass. Jed's on his way with Doctor Addingham — doubtless he'll have to show him the way, for we've never had to call him out before; Mr Lingfield, the apothecary, does very well for us. But as Jed says, you're a lady born, so the doctor it must be, and even if you was to be so bad that you couldn't tell us where you comes from, we could use your pearls to pay his fees.'

The woman rattled on as she fetched a tea tray and proceeded to make tea with as much care as could be seen in any drawing-room.

Verity watched her, too drowsy to think of why she was there. When the tea was ready the woman helped Verity to sit up a little, propping her up against two worn cushions and murmuring anxious apologies that she didn't have goosedown pillows like she was sure to use at home. Verity winced as she tried to put out her hand to take the cup.

Looking down she saw that her left wrist was bruised and swollen.

'Don't be worrying yoursen over that, dearie, Jed thinks 'tis merely a sprain. Here, let me help you with your cup . . .'

Verity sipped at the tea while her dazed mind tried to work out what had happened. She looked at the woman sitting close to the bed, ready to take the cup if Verity's trembling grasp should falter. She had a kindly face, but she was a stranger: Verity had met the majority of Highclough's tenants on her rides on the estate with Luke and she did not recognize the woman. She was about to ask her name when voices were heard approaching the house. Seconds later, the door opened and Verity was momentarily blinded by the glare of winter sunshine that flooded in.

'By God, Mother, 'tis a raw morning!' A big young man clumped into the room, ushering an older man before him and shutting the door firmly against the cold day. 'I've brought Dr Addingham for 'ee, like you said.'

The older man stepped forwards, unwrapping a muffler from his throat and saying in a hearty voice, 'Good day to you, Mistress Gatley. Ah, is that a cup of tea you have there for me? Thank you, ma'am! Now, Jed told me there's been an accident.' His eyes moved towards Verity lying on the settle and he smiled. 'I take it this is the victim. What happened?'

'I — I don't know.'

'Tumbled off her horse,' said the young man called Jed. 'Sailed right over 'is 'ead, she did, and tumbled down the clough, rolling over and over. Came to a stop almost at my feet.'

'Yes, my horse.' Verity frowned, trying to marshal her thoughts. 'Was she hurt? Where is she?'

Jed jerked his thumb towards a small door in the far wall.

'In t'shippon with t'stock. You may be easy, miss, t'mare's well enough.'

'Never mind the mare!' exclaimed Mrs Gatley, jumping up. 'The wonder is that miss here weren't killed! It's a fair drop and no mistake.'

'Bracken,' nodded Jed. 'It weren't burnt off there this year, so there was plenty of old growth to break 'er fall.'

The doctor regarded Verity with a kindly smile.

'Well, it would seem you have been very lucky, miss.' He put down his empty cup and shrugged off his coat. 'Now, let's see if there's any damage, shall we?'

'Aye, and you'll be wanting to be private for that, Doctor.' Mrs Gatley began to hustle her big son towards the door. 'Off you go and feed yon cattle, Jed.' Closing the door upon her son, the good woman settled herself again at her spinning wheel. 'Don't you worry about Gabriel, Doctor: he's busy at his loom and won't be coming down while the light is good.'

'Is that the noise I can hear?' murmured Verity, 'I thought it was in my head.'

'Bless you, miss, that clattering is Mr Gatley at work above stairs!' Mrs Gatley smiled and nodded. 'Now I'll just work in here by the fire and let Dr Addingham get on with his examination.'

'Well,' said that gentleman, a short time later, 'you are an extremely fortunate young woman. There looks to be no bones broken, and nothing more serious than a slight sprain to your wrist.'

'Ah, that's what Jed thought.' From her place beside the hearth Mrs Gatley nodded with satisfaction. 'No sooner had he brought the young lady in than he began wrapping the wrist with cold damp cloths to take down the swelling.'

'And a good job he's made of it, ma'am,' commented the good doctor.

'Aye, well, Jed's used to dealing wit' 'osses,

y'see, and he says it works a treat on strained fetlocks.'

Dr Addingham's eyes twinkled as he looked down at Verity.

'How fortunate that you fell into such — ah — accomplished hands! However, my own recommendation would be that we bind the wrist now, and you do not try to use it for a week or so. And although I can detect no injury to your head, thank Heaven, I think you will begin to feel the effects of your tumble over the next few days, so it would be best for you to remain here quietly for a few days.'

'Oh, but I cannot — Mrs — Mrs Gatley has been most kind, most accommodating, but I am a stranger — '

'Now as to that, miss, don't you be fretting. Father and I'll be glad to have you in the house for a while longer. I'm just thankful we kept the old settle when my mother died, for it's just the thing for 'ee. When Jed brought you in, we only had to bring a mattress down, for I knew it wouldn't do no good to be putting you upstairs, what with Father clacking away on the loom all day, and sometimes Jed too. And don't you be thinking you're putting us out, for we can as easily sit in the kitchen for a couple of evenings, and no bother.'

'Thank you — you are too kind.'

Mrs Gatley blushed rosily and to hide her confusion she turned again to the doctor, pressing him to have more tea. Dr Addingham glanced at the tea-pot, which had been sitting beside the fire for a good half-hour, and gracefully declined. He looked back at Verity.

'Now, miss, perhaps if you are not too tired, you might be able to tell us who you are? No one here knows you, you see, and I regret that you are a stranger to me, also.'

'I am Verity Shore, of Highclough. My horse bolted, and took me out of my way.' She paused as Jed came into the room again. 'I am very grateful that you found me, Mr — Mr Gatley.'

'Aye, 'twas lucky I saw thee fall,' grinned that young man, stripping off his coat. 'The clough is rarely used, and you could be a-lying there still. Right over 'oss's 'ead she went, Doctor.'

That gentleman nodded sagely. 'Spirited animal is she?'

'Not exceptionally so,' said Miss Shore. 'She has never done anything like it before, she has always been so beautifully mannered.'

'Aye, but even the sweetest nature don't take kindly to barbs,' put in young Mr Gatley, warming himself beside the fire. 'There was a piece of metal sticking out o' saddle. Cut right into the poor animal's back. I've been checking her now — it's healing nicely but it'll be some weeks before you can ride her again.'

Verity frowned. 'I don't understand.'

'Well it's a queer do and no mistake,' Jed reached into the pouch hanging from his belt. 'Very careless of the stable lads to overlook this.'

Verity reached out to take the piece of metal and found herself holding a small, sharp arrowhead.

11

As soon as the doctor had departed, one of the farm-hands was despatched to High-clough and Verity lay back against her pillows to await Mrs Worsthorne, whom she was sure would set out immediately to see her. She looked forward to the visit with mixed feelings, aware of the imposition her presence must be to her hosts. She had learned that Mr Gatley and his son earned their living from a combination of weaving and farming, while Mrs Gatley supplemented their earnings with her spinning. All the daylight hours were filled with industry, and the rhythmic thud, thud of the looms working overhead was constant. Verity did not see the master of the house until the short winter day was ending, when Mr Gatley descended to join his wife and son at the dinner-table. He was a tall, spare man with a sober expression, but he spoke in a very civil way to Miss Shore, enquiring after her health and brushing aside her apologies for the inconvenience she must be causing them all.

It was shortly after they had finished dinner that a hasty knock was heard upon the door.

Verity heard Megs's voice and a moment later the widow came hurrying into the room, with Luke close behind her.

Mrs Gatley gave a slight curtsy and awkwardly accepted Mrs Worsthorne's profuse expressions of gratitude while Luke strode across the room and dropped to his knees beside the settle.

'Cousin! Thank God you are safe — are you hurt?'

Verity noted his anxious look and did her best to reassure him. She held up her bandaged arm.

'As you see. Mrs Gatley called out Dr Addingham and he has found nothing worse than a sprained wrist. He says, however, that he would rather I did not travel for a few days.'

'The lad said they found you in the clough.'

'Yes. Delphi bolted, and I was thrown.'

'You could have been killed!' Luke muttered. 'Where is the mare now?'

'She is stabled in the — the shippon, with the cattle. She is perfectly safe,' added Verity, observing his sudden frown.

'But she will be using up valuable winter fodder: I will take her back with me.'

'What, tonight?' Mrs Worsthorne looked up, surprised.

'But, Luke,' said Verity, 'the animals are bedded down for the night, you cannot want to disturb them now.'

'I can assure the young master that the mare is in no one's way,' put in Mr Gatley in his quiet voice. 'And a few days' feed won't harm us.'

Verity looked at Luke, silently begging him not to offend the dignity of her kind host. At length Luke nodded.

'Of course,' he said stiffly. 'I am most obliged to you, Mr Gatley.'

'Verity, you are very pale, my love.' Mrs Worsthorne, peered closely at her cousin.

'I am a little tired, Megs. Pray don't worry. The doctor is confident I need only to rest for a few days.'

'And you are satisfied with him?' asked Luke. 'Perhaps we should call out our own doctor . . .'

'Thank you, Cousin, but I see no need. Doctor Addingham seemed quite competent and he is to call again in two days' time to tell me if I am well enough to go home.'

'If you are to stay then you must let me come over to nurse you!' declared Megs.

Verity resolutely declined her kind offer and in this she was joined by Mrs Gatley who declared that Miss Shore was no trouble at all. A civil but protracted argument then ensued, which was only resolved when it was agreed that Verity's maid should come over every day to assist Mrs Gatley.

'And be assured you're welcome to stay here for as long as Doctor Addingham thinks it right,' said that good woman, twisting her hands together in her apron. 'Lord knows it ain't what you're use to, but . . . '

Mrs Worsthorne made haste to assure her that there was nothing lacking in the cottage, and that she had never before seen such a well-appointed room. She then declined Mrs Gatley's offer of refreshment, saying that they would have to return to Highclough while there was light enough to see their way.

'I mean to come and see you tomorrow, if Mrs Gatley will permit? I shall bring Ella with me — she shall look out some clothes for you, too — and Luke will send the coach at dusk to bring the maid home.' Mrs Worsthorne stood back, pulling on her gloves while Luke leaned over the settle to plant a light kiss on Verity's brow.

'Are you sure there is nothing I can bring you, Cousin?'

'Nothing, thank you. I am very comfortable.'

'Then what ails you, Verity?'

Her eyes flew to his face. 'You think me troubled?' She tried to keep her tone light. 'It is perhaps my dislike of being idle. Will you come again?'

He squeezed her hand.

'Of course. I would stay now, and sleep on the floor if you wish it!'

Her ready smile appeared.

'No, no, that would be most improper! See to your estate work tomorrow, and visit me again after Doctor Addingham's visit — I am hopeful that he will say then that I can go home!'

★   ★   ★

When the visitors had gone, Mrs Gatley made Verity comfortable in her makeshift bed and left her to rest.

'I shall be in the kitchen with Father and Jed, so you only has to call if you want me,' she said, straightening the covers around her patient.

Assuring her that she would sleep, Verity waited until she was alone then reached under her pillow and pulled out the arrowhead. She asked herself why she had not told Luke about it. It was, she thought, because she feared to acknowledge even to herself that it could not have found its way under the saddle by accident. Someone had deliberately tried to harm her.

The next day Verity realized the truth of the doctor's words as she stirred. Her joints ached at every movement, and she was glad to take a little laudanum to help her sleep through the morning. She smiled bravely during Mrs Worsthorne's visit, uttered her thanks for the fresh clothes that the maid had brought with her, but decided she would not get up that day. With Verity dozing on the settle, there was little Ella could do for her, and the maid spent the hours helping Mrs Gatley with household chores. As dusk approached, Ella helped her mistress into a fresh nightgown and tidied her hair before returning to Highclough. It was some time after the gig had collected the maid that the men of the house descended from their looms at the dinner hour. As they passed through the main room they spoke briefly to Miss Shore before making their way to the kitchen while Mrs Gatley helped Verity with her meal.

After dinner, the family settled down in the kitchen and Verity could hear the men's voices drifting through the open door, discussing wool prices, and whether their pieces would be ready to take to the Cloth Hall on Saturday. A clatter of hoofs in the yard and a loud rapping at the door interrupted their conversation. Sleepily, Verity turned her head to see Mr and Mrs Gatley coming out of the kitchen. The woman stood back as her husband put his hand on her arm.

'It's all right, Mother. I'll do it.'

In a leisurely fashion he stepped across to the door and pulled it open. A muffled figure filled the doorway.

'Good evening, Gabriel. I beg your pardon for calling so late.'

Verity's eyes flew open, her pulse began to race as Mr Gatley stood back to let Rafe Bannerman step into the room. His great-coated figure seemed to fill all the space and she felt a hot panic rise and block her throat. She was not ready — she would not see him! If she had been at Highclough, a servant would have announced the visitor and she could have made her excuses, but here in this farmhouse there was no escape, Mrs Gatley was already greeting the visitor warmly, dropping a curtsy and offering him refreshment. He was obviously well known to the family.

'Thank you, ma'am, a cup of Gabriel's home-brewed would be very welcome.' Jed, emerging from the kitchen, was sent back to fetch a tankard of ale for their visitor and Mrs Gatley bustled about Verity, bringing a lamp, plumping up the pillows and putting a shawl about Verity's shoulders before allowing Mr Bannerman to approach. Miss Shore was glad of the few moments' delay as she tried to control the tumult of emotions that this visitor had roused.

'Pray excuse my calling so late,' he repeated, 'but the moon is up, and when I heard you were nursing a young friend of mine . . . '

'You are most welcome, Mr Bannerman,' Mrs Gatley assured him, stepping back from the settle. 'Miss Shore will receive you now.'

Verity clutched nervously at the blanket as the gentleman approached her.

'So, Miss Shore, you tumbled into the clough!' The voice was friendly enough but she could see that he was frowning, black brows drawn together. It was impossible to read his expression.

'Aye, sir. Rolled almost from top to bottom she did.' Jed handed a brimming tankard to Mr Bannerman. The gentleman's eyes did not move from her face.

'You are fortunate to be alive, then. Did you suffer any hurt?'

'No, sir. Merely a few bruises and a sprained wrist.'

'Can you recall what happened?'

'I — no. Delphi bolted and . . . I woke up here.'

'It must have been an ordeal, nevertheless.'

'It could have been much more serious, if young Mr Gatley had not found me.'

Rafe Bannerman turned to the young man. 'You saw what happened?'

'Aye, sir, that I did. I'd been walking in the long pasture, you see, and was just coming back along Clough Bottom when I heard a horse thundering along the cliff top, then all of a sudden she stops, and Miss Shore goes sailing over her head and rolls over and over, down almost to my feet! So I picked her up and fetched her home as quick as I could.'

'And you saw no one else?' Mr Bannerman asked him. 'You're sure of that?'

'Aye, I'm certain of it. There was no one else on the road, I'd have seen 'em.'

'Brigg's horse lost a shoe,' put in Verity. 'Just after we had reached the moor. I left him walking back to Highclough.'

'How unfortunate.'

She put up her chin, fighting off the panic as she forced herself to look at him.

'Yes, Mr Bannerman, it was, wasn't it?'

'And the mare, has the incident given you a dislike of her? Would you like me to take her back to Newlands with me?'

'No! That is, if — if you think Lady Winter

163

would not object, I — I should like to keep her.' She found she could not meet his eyes.

'Sally has already left Newlands, but I am sure she would not object.'

Verity nodded slightly. She wished he would sit down rather than tower over her so menacingly, but he continued to stand. She kept her eyes lowered, her free hand plucking nervously at the covers. Abruptly, he stepped back.

'I am sorry, you are tired and you do not want me here.' He drained his tankard and picked up his hat and gloves from the table. 'I have stayed too long — I came only to assure myself you suffered no serious hurt.'

'Thank you.' Her voice was scarcely above a whisper.

As he turned back towards her she forced herself not to shrink from him but he merely bowed to her before turning once again to his hosts.

'Thank you for letting me see Miss Shore, and again my apologies for disturbing you so late. Oh, and Jed, perhaps you could find a lantern and we will take a look at the mare on the way out . . . '

Verity closed her eyes: she could not protest: he would see the mark on Delphi's back and Jed would explain about the arrowhead in the saddle, tell him that he had given it to her — then Rafe Bannerman would know that she must suspect him.

It was a full week before Dr Addingham allowed Verity to leave the Gatley's farm and when Mrs Worsthorne and her son came to collect her she was able to walk to the coach with only a little help from Luke's supporting arm. As Luke tucked a warm rug about Verity's knees, Mrs Worsthorne reiterated her thanks to Mr and Mrs Gatley, and pressed them again to take some payment for their trouble. The couple were adamant in their refusal but as Mr Worsthorne was about to turn away, Mr Gatley coughed.

'There is one thing, sir . . . I've a young relative coming to stay, a good lad he is, from Brighouse way. Trouble is, he'll be needin' work, and there ain't a right lot here for him to do, for me and Jed sees to it all between us. Besides, he's not a weaver, more used to working with horses.'

'Send him over, we'll find him work in the stables,' said Luke. He glanced at Verity. 'That is, Cousin, if you don't object.'

'No, no, I am only too happy to oblige.' She smiled and held out her hand. 'Goodbye, sir — Mrs Gatley. I shall ride over to see you just as soon as I am able!'

12

A prolonged spell of wet weather precluded any outside activities for the ladies during the next few weeks, giving Miss Shore plenty of time to recover. The weather did not prevent Luke from his regular visits to Halifax or Derringden, but for the ladies the only entertainment to alleviate the monotony was a visit of the packman on his circuitous route from Halifax to Manchester. This individual called upon them one drear afternoon when the ladies were busy with their mending. When Ditton announced the packman's arrival, Verity greeted the diversion with relief and instructed that the fellow should bring his wares into the great hall, where they and the servants might view them in comfort. She recognized the spare figure in the brown coat as the same man she had seen at Bridestones.

'Jason, is it not? So you are back this way already,' she greeted him cheerfully.

'Aye, ma'am, and mighty wet the journey was, though a body still works up a thirst.'

Verity laughed and requested the butler to bring ale for their guest.

'Has Ditton told you that you may stay in

the barn tonight?' she enquired.

'Aye, ma'am, that he has.' The packman touched his fore-lock. 'Though he seemed to think Master Luke wouldn't like it, but I called in at the Eagle in Derringden on my way here, and they was expecting him there this evening. I spotted some very choice spirits there, too, ready to lose a pretty penny at the card table. I doubt if Master Luke'll be home much before the dawn.'

Verity cast an anxious glance at Mrs Worsthorne to see how she received this news, but she was already looking through a selection of lace tippets and trying not to think of her wayward son. The packman continued to talk as he emptied his bags.

'I was very sorry to miss you last time, mistress. Quite a to do there was, with the new Highclough lady lost on the moor. But all's well now, ma'am, is it?'

'Yes, very well,' returned Verity, sorting through the ribbons he had spread across the wide oak table.

'The stable lad was saying you came off with nothing worse than a sprained wrist.'

'Yes, and even that is almost recovered — Mrs Gatley insisted on wrapping my wrist in cold, wet cloths to take away the inflammation.'

'I cannot see why she should have done so,

when you were chilled to the bone to begin with!' declared Mrs Worsthorne, picking out a comb with a decorated handle.

The packman did not reply immediately, for the butler handed him a tankard of small-beer and he took a long draught, smacking his lips in appreciation.

'I've heard the cold treatment works, ma'am,' he said at last in his slow drawl. 'The colder the better to take down the swelling and relieve the pain — and they do say 'tis the same with a burn. Wrap it in linen soaked in cold water, and keep putting on a fresh cold dressing to take away the heat.' He tipped out the contents of another bag, scattering a rainbow of sewing threads beside the ribbons. 'I even heard tell that when the Blue Bell Inn at Otley caught fire last winter, the landlord was burned something terrible, but there was a guest at the inn, a scholarly gentleman who had spent many years in the East and he made the landlord lie in the snow. Then he kept on packing fresh snow around 'un for an hour or more, and the poor man recovered with barely a scar.' The packman nodded slowly at the ladies, then drained his tankard and turned back to the business in hand. 'Now I've some pieces of the finest Norwich silk if you ladies was wishing to see them — big enough to hem, and mayhap add a fringe to make a fine shawl . . . '

It was a few more days before the rain cleared, but as soon as the yard was dry Verity made her way to the stables to check on the mare. She found Luke there, talking to Brigg, but at her approach he dismissed the groom, who walked quickly away without looking at Miss Shore.

'Good morning, Cousin. I am riding into Derringden, do you have an errand for me?'

'No, thank you. I have all I need.'

He looked hard at her. 'You are not riding today, I trust?'

Verity glanced down at her flowered muslin gown with a wry smile.

'Not in this dress! My riding habit was so torn when I came off that I have had to throw it away. Your Mama has asked Madam Juliet to make me a new one. No, I have come to see how Delphi goes on.'

'Come and see for yourself.'

As they crossed the yard, Verity saw a tow-headed young man coming out of the barn that housed the carriages.

'Is that Mr Gatley's young relative?' she asked. Luke nodded.

'Yes. Will Barber. He's a good worker, seems to know his job. Brigg says he's a quiet lad.'

She thought of Brigg's taciturn manner and smiled, but said nothing. Luke walked with Verity into the stable and opened the door of the mare's loose-box, standing back for her to precede him.

'The lads are keeping her exercised on a leading rein, but I think she's missing you.' He grinned as the mare snuffled against Verity's shoulder.

'Poor lady,' she murmured, running her hand over the smooth neck, then on to the animal's back, stopping at the large patch of dried blood.

'We thought it best not to put a saddle on her yet.' Luke was standing behind her and, as he spoke, he reached past her to cover her hand with his own. 'What do you know of this cut on her back, Cousin?'

She swallowed.

'There was a barb under the saddle. That is why Delphi bolted. It — it could not have been an accident . . . '

His fingers tightened over her hand.

'And who do you suspect?' She shook her head and he continued roughly, 'Do you mean you do not know, or that you do not want to face it?'

'Pray, Luke, do not ask me!'

'You could have been killed, Verity! Think! Who would gain from that?'

His free hand moved around her waist, pulling her back against him.

'Marry me, Cousin.' She felt his breath on her cheek. 'As my wife you would be safe, I could take care of you.'

For a heartbeat she considered his offer. The thought of being cared for was an attractive one. She longed to lean back against him, to share her worries, but even in that brief moment she knew that she would be marrying Luke for the wrong reasons. Stifling a sigh she gently released herself from his clasp.

'You are very kind, Luke, and I am sincerely attached to you, but — '

'You will not marry me.'

'No.'

There was a clatter of hoofs in the yard and Verity looked round to see Rafe Bannerman leading his horse into the stable. Verity sprang away from Luke, blushing furiously.

'I appear to be very much *de trop*,' murmured Mr Bannerman.

'I — um — we were not expecting you,' Verity muttered.

'That much is evident. I did send word of my coming, but perhaps you have not seen Ditton this morning.'

'No, not since breakfast.' She tried to sound unconcerned as she stepped out of the loose-box. Luke followed her.

'Have you come to remove the mare, Bannerman?' he asked, 'After all, your horses have not proved very lucky for our family, have they?'

Verity became aware of the sudden tension. A glance at Rafe Bannerman showed her the blazing anger in his face. However, when he spoke, his voice was cool enough.

'I believe Miss Shore is still in need of a horse. However, it occurred to me that you might like me to send over one of my lads to lend a hand in the stables — '

'Thank you, but we already have an extra boy,' Luke interrupted him. 'Will Barber, a relative of Gabriel Gatley — he's a handy lad in the stables and seems to know his job.'

Mr Bannerman shrugged. 'As you wish. Miss Shore, may I escort you to the house?'

'I'll come with you!' put in Luke.

Verity shook her head at him. 'There is no need. You are going out, are you not? And I have already delayed you.'

Luke hesitated. 'Very well,' he said at last. 'Remember, Cousin, Brigg is in the yard if you need him.' He turned towards Mr Bannerman. 'If you will excuse me, I am riding over to the Greenwoods,' he muttered, straining to be civil. 'If you leave your horse here, Rafe, I'll get Will to unsaddle him for you.'

'Shall we see you at dinner, Luke?' asked Verity.

'Pray give my apologies to Mama — I am promised to dine with Sam Greenwood. We have business to discuss.' With a curt nod, Luke strode away. Verity stared after him, a faint crease on her brow.

'Your cousin spends a great deal of time with young Mr Greenwood,' observed Mr Bannerman.

'And why not, when they are of an age?'

Verity turned to walk back towards the house and Mr Bannerman fell into step beside her.

'Why not indeed, except that one is the idle son of a wealthy wool-trader, the other a young man who should be attending to his estates.'

'My cousin works very hard at High-clough!'

'Put away the claws, Miss Shore, I have no criticism of the way he runs your property: it is his own inheritance that he is neglecting.'

Verity bit back a retort, knowing there was some justification in his words. After a moment, Mr Bannerman spoke again.

'Today, however, I am glad he is gone, for it gives me the opportunity to talk to you, alone.' She tensed as she heard the serious note in his voice. 'What have you done with the arrowhead?'

Verity stopped. Her heart jumped to her throat, but she managed a shaky laugh.

'I should have expected a direct attack from you! How did you know?'

'Jed Gatley described the barb he found wedged beneath Delphi's saddle. And before you ask, I have no doubt that it is mine. All the archery equipment is stored in the stable block.' He turned towards her, holding her gaze with his own hard stare. 'Do you really think I tried to kill you?'

She looked away. 'I don't know.'

'Honest, if not complimentary! How little you regard me.'

Hot tears burned her eyelids. Fighting for control, she began to hurry towards the house.

'Now I have hurt you. Damnation!' He caught her arm. 'Verity, look at me. Look at me!' He swung her round, gripping her shoulders. '*I did not* plant that barb.'

Blinking away her tears, Verity lifted her eyes to his face. At last she relaxed slightly, and a faint sigh escaped her.

'No, I don't believe you did.'

'Thank God!' He released her shoulders, but only to take her arm as they continued towards the house. 'Since Jed told me what had happened I have been in daily expectation of receiving a letter from you, forbidding me to come to Highclough.'

'Under the terms of my grandfather's will that would make things very difficult. Besides' — her irrepressible humour peeped through — 'I could not believe you would use such a clumsy method of dispatching me.'

'Nor such an unreliable one.'

She threw another quick glance at him and decided to risk another question.

'Sir, what did Luke mean when he said that your horses were unlucky for the family?'

For a moment she thought he would not answer her, but after a long pause he spoke, as if forcing the words out.

'Your uncle Evelyn was riding one of my horses when he had his accident.' He felt her instinctive recoil and immediately released her arm, although they continued to walk on together. 'His own horse had cast a shoe on the road to Newlands, so we put his saddle on one of my hunters. We had been out less than an hour when Evelyn was unseated and took a tumble. It looked no worse than either of us had experienced before, but on this occasion Evelyn . . . broke his neck.'

'I am very sorry,' Verity replied at last. 'I think you told me once that you and my uncle were close friends. How much worse then that you should feel responsible for his death.'

'Your cousin would like you to believe there is a pattern.' The anger in his voice was not lost on Verity. She slipped her hand through his arm again, wanting to comfort him.

'Luke? No, I am sure you are wrong. I know he is impetuous and . . . and perhaps a little over-protective of me! I think — ' She broke off, frowning.

'Yes, Miss Shore? What do you think? Tell me.'

Verity bit her lip, unwilling to voice her fears. At last she said, 'I think it was Brigg who put the barb under my saddle! After all, he was in the stable block all the time I was at Newlands, and his horse went lame so conveniently on the homeward stretch.'

'And why should he want to harm you, Miss Shore?'

She wrinkled her nose.

'I'm not quite sure, but I suspect that he is . . . jealous of me! He always seems ill at ease when he is with me, and he is devoted to my cousin. I think he does not like me, you see. I have not mentioned it before, but now I have put it into words, it seems a valid explanation.'

'So what will you do?'

'I shall talk to Luke about it as soon as he returns this evening.'

They had reached the house and Mr Bannerman held the door for his companion to enter.

'Just one thing,' he said quietly as she moved past him. 'Take care never to be alone, Miss Shore.'

'But why? That should not be necessary now.'

'If you are abroad, make sure you are accompanied by Megs, or your maid — or that new man, Gatley's relative.'

'But surely, once Luke has been told about Brigg — '

He gripped her wrist. 'Promise me!'

Her eyes flew to his face, questioning, but he said no more. With a little sigh she nodded.

'Very well, sir. I will try.'

'Good girl. Now, I had best get to work. I will come and find you again before I leave.' He strode away, leaving Verity alone in the south passage, aware that her wrist was burning from his rough grasp.

⋆ ⋆ ⋆

Luke did not return until late that night, so it was the following day before Verity could voice her concerns about Brigg. They were alone in the morning-room, and she was not surprised at his incredulous reaction.

'My dear cousin, Brigg has been with me for years! He is a loyal servant!'

'Indeed, I have no doubt that he is loyal to *you*. But think, Luke. He was nowhere to be found shortly before the chimney stone fell into the garden — Rafe was obliged to take the horses to the stable himself. And as for the barb under Delphi's saddle, he would have seen Rafe putting away the archery targets so he knew where everything was stored. It would have been the work of a moment for him to pick up an arrowhead and put it under the saddle.' She saw his frown and added gently, 'I know you do not wish to believe it, but I think Brigg's devotion to you is too powerful. Perhaps he sees me as a threat to you.'

'No, Cousin. I am sure you are wrong. You have no proof, no *real* proof.'

'No, none, but I don't trust him: I cannot be easy while he is at Highclough.'

She ended with an appeal, and seeing her earnest look he shrugged.

'I think you are mistaken, Cousin, but if it will make you happy I will send him away. After all, Highclough will be yours shortly, and you must be assured of the loyalty of your servants. I will talk to him now.'

'Will you dismiss him?'

'No. I shall send him to Sowerby.' He summoned a smile and put his hand briefly on her arm. 'Don't look so anxious, Cousin. If his presence unnerves you, of course Brigg cannot stay here.'

'Thank you.' She paused. 'Luke, what you said about Highclough being mine soon — in less than a month I shall have to take charge of the estate. You have been very helpful in guiding me about the area and introducing me to the tenants, but we have scarcely touched on the accounts.'

'My poor cousin, are you so lost for occupation that you want to do so?' he laughed at her. 'Rest assured, you will pick it up easily enough, and then wish the task on another, for it is mighty tedious!'

He lounged out and she did not see him again until dinner-time when he informed her that Brigg had quit Highclough. The servants had left the room and Megs, to whom Verity had confided her suspicions, shook her head as she helped herself to a slice of lamb.

'A sad business. I suppose Brigg denies it?'

'Of course, Mama, but the only other person with access to the stables that afternoon was Rafe Bannerman, and our cousin will not hear a word against him.'

Verity frowned at this, but it was Mrs Worsthorne who answered.

'Well, of course, he would never do such a thing, my son! Rafe Bannerman is no more capable of such an act than you would be! No, if Brigg is not involved, then I can only think it was a silly prank carried out by one of Rafe's stable hands.'

The entry of Ditton and the footman with the next course put an end to their discussion, and Verity could not be sorry, for she wanted only to put the whole incident behind her.

13

Despite her conviction that Brigg had placed the barb in Delphi's saddle, Verity was aware of a feeling of anxiety when Mr Bannerman invited her to ride out with him a week later, and she was pleased to have the new groom, Will Barber, in attendance. They set out from Highclough under a clear April sky.

Mr Bannerman's invitation had arrived the day after she received her new riding habit, and Verity's curiosity to learn how he had achieved such impeccable timing overcame the slight reserve she felt in the gentleman's presence. In answer to her direct question he merely shrugged.

'Since the seamstress sent the previous reckoning to me, she naturally assumed the same applied on this occasion.'

'Oh, I had not thought — ' She flushed. 'I understood the habit was to be a present from Megs.'

'Your cousin was certainly very willing to pay, but I have assured her that your estate can stand the cost.' He ran an appraising eye over her. 'It's a good choice, Miss Shore, the blue suits you. It is a little plain, perhaps, but you prefer the practical style, do you not?'

'Thank you. I admit I do not like too much lace and fancy embellishment, however feminine.'

He looked at her, a disquieting gleam in his hard eyes.

'That outfit accentuates all your feminine points, Miss Shore, never fear!'

Blushing furiously, Verity kicked her horse on, leading the way at a canter along the grassy lane. The fresh breeze helped to cool her cheeks, and as she checked the mare's pace she felt sufficiently at ease again to enquire after Lady Winter.

'I have today received a letter from my brother-in-law,' he told her, as he came alongside. 'Sir Robin tells me Sally has delivered a fine baby boy — Marcus.'

'Oh I am so pleased! And your sister — she is well?'

'Very well! Robin tells me they are having difficulty making her rest.'

'I am delighted for her. Would you give her my best wishes when you write again?'

'Perhaps you would like to write to her yourself, Miss Shore. I know Sally would be grateful for a letter from you, and I would very much like you to be friends. I will give you her direction when we return.'

Verity flushed and thanked him, conscious

of an unreasonable satisfaction that he should desire her friendship with his sister.

★ ★ ★

They were high on the open moors before he spoke again.

'The mare's back has healed well, I take it?' commented Mr Bannerman.

'Yes. I have ridden her on a few occasions now and she seemed to be suffering no ill effects.'

'Good. Then I hope you are ready for a strenuous ride, Miss Shore.'

'Oh? Where are we going, sir?'

'You'll see.' He urged his horse forward and Verity could only follow, intrigued.

They followed the lane northwards until the walled fields gave way to open moors and the path was picked out by a double row of causey stones that swept in a huge arc around the edge of a wooded valley. At length Mr Bannerman reined in and waited for Verity to catch up with him.

'Have you been this way before?'

'Only once, with Luke, although I believe this is still Highclough land?'

He nodded. 'The moors provide only rough summer grazing. Ambrose always considered this the least profitable part of the estate.' He pointed to the woods. 'What I want to show you is down there, in Beech Clough.'

He turned his horse on to a grassy track that led down through the trees. Verity followed, allowing her mare to pick her way over the uneven ground. As they descended, the trees closed about them and the pleasant smell of the damp earth hung in the air. New green leaves providing a dappled canopy against the bright sun while birds sang freely from the higher branches. The path turned at the edge of a steep ridge where the ground fell away sharply and Verity found herself looking out of the trees into a steep-sided valley. Neat green pastures covered the higher slopes on the far side and a dark line of stone walls divided the farmland from the steep wooded slopes that led down to the valley bottom.

'Oh, how pretty!'

'Derringden and Halifax are that way, to the east.' Following Mr Bannerman's raised arm she observed how the valley wound its way around interlocking spurs of land, small farmsteads dotting the gentler slopes. 'Do you see the cloth stretched out on the tenters to dry?'

'Yes. They look like white sails.'

Her companion grinned.

'Very poetic! Weaving is carried out in each of those houses, but they are restricted by how much yarn their women can spin: it takes more than a dozen spinners to keep three weavers in work. Imagine how much more efficient it would be if we had a manufactory, here in the valley, to spin the yarn!'

She turned to him, smiling at the enthusiasm glowing in his look.

'This is the project Mr Oldroyd talked of at your party.'

'Yes.'

'And is this where you want to build your mill?'

'Yes, down here. Come on.'

They set off again, descending once again through woodland. The path finally came to an end and Verity looked about her: they were in a small clearing with the merry sound of water rushing near at hand.

'Well, Mr Bannerman, what is it you want me to see?'

'We must go the rest of the way on foot. Will you come?'

He dismounted and walked across to her, holding up his hands. Verity kicked her foot free from the stirrup and dropped into his arms. His hold tightened and Verity was shocked at the pleasure she experienced being held so close to a man. Blushing for her thoughts, she dared not look up and was aware of a mixture of relief and regret when, a moment later, he released her. With a word to the groom to stay with the horses, he took Verity by the hand and led her through the trees, picking the easiest route across the rock-strewn valley. At last the water was in sight, a tumbling white froth that roared over its rocky bed. Mr Bannerman stopped.

'The finest water in the county, and a good descent to add to its power.'

Verity laughed. 'Of course. For your water frame!'

'Exactly. But it is not just mine, there are several others, businessmen and landowners keen to invest in the idea. Josiah Sutcliffe owns the land on the other side of the valley, then there is Amos Williams — and James Oldroyd, whom you know.'

'All men of substance, I believe.'

'Indeed. Very well then! With your permission, we could build the mill here to take advantage of the constant water supply. We will collect the tops — that is, the best of the wool — from the local woolcombers, spin it here and then return it to the weavers. We calculate we can provide enough wool to keep every weaver in the district busy all year!'

She smiled at the enthusiasm in his voice.

'You think it is viable? It seems so, so remote here.'

'Not only viable, imperative! The manufacturers of Manchester and Bradford will soon be producing more cloth than we can ever hope to do if we continue in the present piecemeal fashion. They will not come so far to collect their cloth if it has to be trailed all over the country by mule. The track leading up to the causeway would have to be improved, of course, but we would also open up a toll road along the valley bottom to Derringden, where we can pick up the new canal — that will give us access to Rochdale and Manchester. We must make use of it, or see the people leaving the hills to find employment in the towns.'

'And would you employ children, as Sir Richard does in Cromford?' Verity asked, frowning. 'The mills there operate day and night, and I have watched the little children going into work; they look so pale . . . '

'Children are a good source of cheap labour,' he reminded her.

'But it cannot be right, sir! They are little more than babies!'

'I will employ no child under ten, Miss Shore, you may depend on that.'

She turned to look at him, her anxious eyes searching his face.

'Truly?'

'You have my word.'

She looked back at the water, tumbling and frothing over its rocky bed.

'It could work,' she murmured. 'The valley widens considerably from this point, so there would be room here for small houses too, like those at Cromford, and even a school.'

'There are other valleys, of course, but none with such a good source of water.'

'And a new toll road would link it with the canal, too.'

'Exactly!' He looked down at her. 'What do you say, Miss Shore? In a couple of weeks you will be mistress of Highclough and able to make your own decision. Will you sell the valley to us?'

Verity gazed at the stream, imagining its power harnessed and a complex of stone buildings filling the valley. She felt the first stirrings of excitement.

'No, I think not.'

His black brows drew together. 'No? You dislike the idea?'

'I think,' she said slowly, 'I would prefer to keep it, and join you as a business partner.'

'A partner! I never thought — ' He laughed. 'Of course! Why not?' He turned to face her, his hands on her shoulders. 'You are an unusual woman, Verity Shore!'

'No, merely a sensible one. If there are profits to be made, why should Highclough not share them?'

'If it's fast profits you are looking for, Miss Shore, then you will have to use the children. We are not looking for a quick return on this investment.'

'No more am I. But I will insist that you build a school here.'

As she smiled up at him, his grip on her shoulders tightened and there was a blazing look in his hard eyes that she could not read. Her heart seemed to leap into her throat, suffocating her. She felt sick and faint and strangely elated all at once, and it frightened her. Fixing her eyes on the top button of his coat, she tried to speak normally.

'P-perhaps you will ask Mr Reedley to draw up the papers. We will need a legal contract for this.'

'What? Oh, yes.' Abruptly he let her go and turned away. 'We should go back. Megs will think I have kidnapped you!'

He strode off ahead of her, his pale greatcoat flapping about him. Verity sighed a little and shook her head, wondering if he had been as shaken as she by the moment they had just shared, or perhaps he was angered because she proposed to join him in his mill-building venture.

Far from worrying, Mrs Worsthorne greeted them serenely.

'I guessed you would be gone all afternoon and I have had dinner put back an hour. You will join us, Master Rafe?'

The gentleman cast a swift glance at his companion.

'If Miss Shore is not sick of my company by now, I would be delighted.'

★　★　★

'So, Bannerman has been explaining his dream to you, Cousin.' Mr Worsthorne lounged back from the table and pushed his fair hair back from his brow. 'I hope he has not persuaded you to invest in his ridiculous schemes.'

Mrs Worsthorne shifted uncomfortably, but Mr Bannerman merely smiled.

'Why ridiculous, Luke?'

'Well, anyone can see that this new-fangled machinery won't work.'

'Believe me, it is the future — '

'The future? Aye, and so it may be, if you want a future where the people are put out of work by machines! How is a man to earn his keep if a machine can do his job in half the time?'

'The weavers will continue with their

looms and their farms. Others can work in the manufactory. I want to keep worsted production in the area, Luke. Others will embrace this change even if we do not.'

Luke drained his glass and reached for the bottle.

'The men will rise up and destroy your machines, Rafe, when they see them taking away their work!' he growled. 'It is already happening in Manchester. If my cousin will heed my advice she will have nothing to do with this!'

Verity was silent, and Mr Bannerman gave her a reassuring smile.

'I think we can leave Miss Shore to decide for herself.'

* * *

Mr Bannerman left soon after, by which time Luke had already broached his third bottle. Mrs Worsthorne eyed her son anxiously as she bade him goodnight, and Verity was about to follow the widow out of the drawing-room when Mr Worsthorne called her back.

'Damned impostor! How dare he try to persuade you to join in his madcap schemes!'

Verity carefully closed the door upon the wooden-faced butler crossing the hall.

'I do not think it so outrageous, Cousin. I

believe it could provide Highclough with much-needed income.'

He pushed back his chair and lounged to the window, staring into the blackness.

'Ha! Rafe has sweet-talked you into thinking his way!'

She laughed and came back to the table.

'I have never heard any *sweet-talk* from Mr Bannerman! But his arguments were convincing, and there are several like-minded men willing to join in the venture, including Mr Oldroyd, whom you know.'

Luke scowled.

'So when you are mistress here you will hand over the valley to him?'

'I do not intend to hand over anything. I wish to be a partner and have a full say in this business. I shall speak to Mr Oldroyd, then discuss the matter thoroughly with Mr Reedley. Pray believe that I will not rush into this, Luke.'

She moved back towards the door but her cousin forestalled her, crossing the room to lay his hand on the door just as she reached it.

'Cousin — Verity! Verity, my dear, don't go!'

'Luke, what is it?' She looked up at him, frowning. 'What is it you wish to say to me?' She could smell the fumes of wine and brandy on his breath and she stepped away from him, waiting for him to continue.

'Cousin — Cousin, I didn't mean to speak again, but I cannot let this pass! Pray, my dear, I cannot let you take on this house and its land on your own, with no one to guide you.'

'No, of course I understand that, and I appreciate your efforts in showing me over the estate — '

'No! That's not enough!' He turned away, running his fingers through his hair. 'Cousin, Highclough is not an easy place to live. The land is poor and the climate savage. It is no place for you to be alone.'

'Luke — '

'No, let me finish!' He came up to her and took her hands. 'Cousin, I know you do not love me yet, but that could change: an alliance between us could be very profitable — I *know* this land, I love it! Together we could manage it, improve the farms, increase the rents — there would be no need to build new mills, destroying all that is best about this place!'

'Luke, hush now. Please believe me, I am minded to allow the mill to be built in Beech Clough, but will do nothing until I have spoken with Mr Reedley. As to the other, well, I have told you I cannot marry you, but

I shall always value your advice.'

'Yet now, when I give you my view, you fly directly against it!'

'No, I have said I shall think on it.' She put up her hand to smooth the hair from his brow. 'Please, Luke. Be my friend on this.'

'Friend! I would be your husband!'

'I know, and I am honoured, but . . . I cannot.'

'Is it Bannerman?' he demanded. 'Damn him. Has Rafe been making love to you?'

'Of course not!' She knew her flushed cheeks betrayed her, but she answered him frankly. 'I — I am not even sure that he likes me. But that is beside the point, Luke. I want us to be friends, I *need* you for my friend.' She met his gaze steadily, observing in his face the emotions battling within him. For a moment she thought the anger in him would win and he would strike out at her, but she stood her ground and was relieved to see the passion leave him. Finally he nodded.

'I am . . . thankful for your friendship, Cousin.' With a stiff bow he turned away, yanking open the door and striding off across the hall.

★ ★ ★

The first day of May saw the annual fair in Derringden. Mrs Worsthorne gave the servants leave to go and enjoy themselves, and the ladies sat down to a cold luncheon in the quiet house. They had just finished their meal when Mr Bannerman appeared.

'Pray don't get up! I merely looked in to tell you that I had arrived. Reedley has asked me to sort out some papers for one of the tenancies.' His dark glance swept across Verity, not meeting her eyes. 'I shall be in the office most of the afternoon.'

Verity's spirits sank. The dismissal was all too clear. Since their ride to the valley Rafe Bannerman had not been near Highclough, and she cudgelled her brain for an explanation, going back over their conversation, scrutinizing every word, every look. She thought she had seen something in his eyes that mirrored her own heart, but it could not be so, or he would not be so cold now. The afternoon dragged on and Verity could settle to nothing. Her plans for the shrubbery had still not been drawn up and she took her sketch pad out into the garden, determined to make progress. However, after the third spoiled drawing she threw down her pad and pencil and marched to the door leading to the office passage. To her frustration, the door was locked and she was forced to walk back around the house to the main entrance. She noted that Mr Bannerman's greatcoat and curly-brimmed beaver were still hanging outside his office and, taking a deep breath, she knocked and went in.

Rafe Bannerman was sitting at the desk, staring at a sheaf of papers. Upon her entry he looked up, frowning. Verity twisted her fingers together and forced herself to look at him.

'Sir, you will tell me, if you please, what I have done that has so offended you?'

The black brows went up. 'Why should you think I am offended?'

'You have not been near me since our ride to Beech Clough. If I said — did — anything then . . . '

'You should not be here.'

She winced at his harsh tone.

'I know — I am sorry, but I cannot bear you to think that I was . . . forward.'

Mr Bannerman stood up and came towards her.

'You were perfectly adorable.'

'Oh. Then what — '

Her words were cut short as the gentleman pulled her to him and kissed her roughly. Shock immobilized her for a few seconds, then her arms crept around his neck and she found herself responding. When at last he raised his head she made no effort to move away, but leaned against him, her head on his shoulder.

'Oh,' she sighed, 'I should not have done that.'

His arms tightened about her and she felt his cheek pressing on her head.

'I know it! That is the reason I have been so distant, my dear heart, because until this damned business is wound up I have no right to treat you thus. That day in Beech Clough you looked up at me so trustingly I wanted to sweep you up and make love to you on the spot.'

She shivered delightfully.

'Then I wish you had told me as much. I have been perfectly miserable since then, thinking that you were angry with me.'

'My poor darling!' He dropped a light kiss on her hair, then, cupping her chin with his lean fingers he tilted her face towards him and brushed her mouth with his lips. 'Bear with me,' he murmured. 'Once you are mistress here I promise you I shall come courting you with all the pomp and ceremony I can muster.'

She gave him a misty smile.

'That will not be necessary, but if it pleases you . . .'

He kissed her again, then put her away from him.

'It *pleases* me! Now go away, my dear. Once I have sorted these papers everything will be in order for Reedley to pass over to you on your birthday, but I cannot work with you here to distract me!'

'Very well, sir. How long should it take you?'

'A couple of hours, no more.'

Verity looked towards the window. 'With this heavy cloud it is already getting dark. Megs has put dinner back an hour to give Luke time to get back from Halifax: will you not take dinner with us and stay here tonight?'

The look in his eyes brought a blush to her cheeks.

'You want to torture me further by making me sleep under the same roof as you? Very well, cruel one, tell Ditton to set another place at dinner!'

★ ★ ★

As if in a dream, Verity floated out of the office. She ran upstairs to fetch her spencer then made her way outside, planning to walk round to the shrubbery and collect her sketch book. However, the temptation to go the long way, to pass the office window and peep in was overwhelming. She cupped her hands around her face and peered through the glass. The movement attracted Mr Bannerman's attention, and he waved her away, scowling, but this only made Verity laugh, and she blew him a kiss before skipping away towards the shrubbery. Picking up her sketch pad and pencil, Verity made one final attempt to begin her sketch. She was pleased with her progress, but the light was fading fast. The grey cloud which had shut out the sun for most of the day now descended, shrouding Highclough in a thick, damp mist. Verity packed away her pencils and was about to leave the shrubbery when she heard her name. Looking up, she saw a figure standing at the end of the walk, a tall figure in a high-crowned beaver and a white caped driving coat. She laughed.

'Rafe! What on earth — '

He put his finger to his lips, and beckoned her to follow him. With a smile and a shake of her head, Verity made her way along the walk. She could feel the droplets of water from the mist clinging to her hair.

'Are we going far, Rafe, because I have no cloak . . . '

He ignored her, striding away so that she

had to run to keep him in sight. He slipped through a small gate at the end of the shrubbery and marched across the field that bordered the stable block. He glanced back occasionally to make sure Verity was following, but did not slacken the pace.

'Rafe, wait!' she cried. The long grass was damp and soon her thin sandals were saturated. They were out of sight of the house now, at the very edge of the gardens, and the conical mound of the ice house was before them. Verity saw the tail of Rafe's white coat disappear around the mound and she hurried to follow him. As she rounded the ice house she was surprised to see that the heavy outer door was open. Peering into the darkness, she could see the white blur of the driving coat in the passage.

'Now what game is this, sir? Why all the intrigue?' She stepped into the tunnel, straining her eyes to see. Rafe was before her and she heard the scrape and creak of the inner door as she approached. She stepped up beside him. 'Why are we here — Oh!' He suddenly grabbed her and as she opened her mouth to protest a soft ball of cloth was forced between her teeth. Verity felt herself lifted off the ground and the next moment she was tumbling into the darkness of the ice pit. Her fall was broken by the thick layer of straw that covered the ice, but as she scrambled to her feet she heard the door creaking shut above her, and a moment later she was in complete darkness.

14

'Rafe! Rafe!' Verity pulled the cloth from her mouth and screamed. Above the echo of her cries she heard the outer door thud. She knew her eyes were open, but the darkness was like black velvet, with no chink of light. She reached out her hands and felt the smooth side of the pit. Stretching up as far as possible she still could not feel the top ledge. Shaking, she sank down on to the straw, trying to subdue her panic while she considered her situation. She had been thrown into the ice house to die! Mixed with her fear there was boiling anger: Rafe had led her into the trap; he had forcibly thrown her into the pit. This time there could be no mistake!

'What a fool I have been!' she muttered, blinking back her tears. The straw beneath her scratched her hands and, as she shifted her position, her fingers fell on the soft ball of material that had been pressed into her mouth. In the darkness she explored the square of silk — a handkerchief, perhaps? She pulled it through her fingers, feeling the raised embroidery thread in one corner.

Swiftly she pushed the handkerchief into her pocket: it was most likely that Rafe's initials were embroidered on to the silk, and if she was going to die she hoped it might explain who had murdered her. Pushing aside such morbid thoughts, she rose to her feet and began to explore the walls of the ice pit. They were smooth brick, with not so much as a handhold. When she thought she must be back where she started, she sank down again, calculating how long it would be before she was found. This part of the gardens was seldom used. There would be no more ice this year to add to their stock, and the first time Cook would require ice would be to make the sorbet for her birthday dinner in two weeks' time.

Panic welled up within her and she began to shout and scream until her lungs ached and she fell sobbing on to the straw. She knew her efforts were useless, the thick walls and double doors would muffle all sound.

Verity stifled the urge to cry. That would do no good at all. She scrambled to her knees and in the darkness she began to pull the loose straw towards her until she had fashioned a nest around her, then curled up under the scratchy covering to await her fate.

★ ★ ★

Mrs Worsthorne was crossing the great hall just as Mr Bannerman appeared from the office passage. Even in the dim candlelight her anxiety was evident.

'Rafe, is my cousin with you?'

'Miss Shore? No, I have not seen her for two hours or more.'

'Strange.' She frowned. 'Her maid tells me she has not been to her room to change for dinner.'

'Perhaps she is already in the drawing-room.'

'No, I have come from there in search of her.'

Mr Bannerman followed the widow to the dining-room, but that too was empty.

'Could she be with Luke?'

Mrs Worsthorne shook her head.

'One of the village lads has brought me word that he is dining in Derringden, which is most vexing, when he knew I was setting dinner back especially for him! If ever anyone was so tiresome! That is why I was looking for Verity, to tell her that we need not wait dinner after all.'

Mr Bannerman was frowning at the dining-table.

'Only two places are set.'

Mrs Worsthorne looked round, distracted. 'Yes, I told Ditton to remove Luke's place, since he will not be joining us.'

The gentleman's hard eyes moved to her face.

'Then Verity did not tell him I would be joining you.'

'Will you? We shall be glad of your company on such a gloomy evening. I have had Ditton light a fire in the drawing-room to cheer us all.'

'Then it is possible she did not come back into the house . . . have the stables been checked?'

'No, but she never rides out alone now, and Will Barber has gone off to the fair today, with the other servants.'

'Nevertheless, I will look in the stables, and the garden.'

Mrs Worsthorne waited impatiently for his return, but when he came back his grim look did nothing to reassure her, and she clasped her hands together in an anxious supplication.

'Oh heavens, where can she be?'

Those servants who had returned from the fair were summoned and while Mrs Worsthorne undertook a thorough search of the house, Rafe Bannerman went out with the footmen to search the grounds. He returned some time later to find Mrs Worsthorne in the great hall, pacing anxiously before the window. He held up a sketch pad.

'I found this in the shrubbery, but there was no sign of Miss Shore.' He shrugged off his driving coat and threw it over a chair. 'One of the men has taken a lantern and is checking the lane, but it is too dark to do more tonight. We will go out again at first light. You look tired, ma'am. Ditton tells me dinner is ready. I suggest we try to eat something.'

'I could not manage a crumb!' declared the widow tearfully. 'I vow I do not know which way to turn! If only Luke was here — why must he choose tonight to stay out with his friends!'

Mr Bannerman took her arm. 'Come, ma'am, it will do no good if we starve ourselves. We will need our strength for later.' He guided Mrs Worsthorne to the dining-room and coaxed her to take a little soup and a few slices of chicken. However, neither of them touched the cheesecake or the sweet-meats, and Ditton was about to remove the dishes when there was the unmistakable sound of a door banging. Without a word Mrs Worsthorne hurried from the room with Mr Bannerman close behind her. As they entered the great hall Mr Worsthorne appeared from the office passage.

'Luke! Thank heaven you are here, my son!'

The gentleman stopped. His coat and waistcoat were unbuttoned, and his tousled hair fell forward over his brow. He swayed slightly as he tried to fix his gaze upon his mother.

'As you see, Mama.' He continued on his way and she followed him into the drawing-room.

'Luke, we are in such a worry! Verity has disappeared, and . . . ' She trailed off, a frown creasing her brow as she watched her son move unsteadily to the sideboard and pick up a decanter. 'Luke, my dear, do you think perhaps you have had enough brandy for one evening?'

Luke ignored her while he filled a glass, then turned, giving his mother a sullen stare.

'D'you think I can't take my drink, Mama?' His over-bright eyes shifted to Mr Banner-man and his lip curled. 'You still here, Rafe? You seem to be making yourself quite at home!'

'Perhaps you did not understand, Luke. Miss Shore is missing.'

'Gone, is she? Most likely she has run away to escape your attentions.' Luke gulped down the brandy and refilled his glass. 'Don't think

I ain't aware that you've been trying to win her favour.' He jabbed an accusing finger towards Mr Bannerman. 'Highclough would make a tidy little addition to your property, would it not?'

'Luke that is enough!' Mrs Worsthorne said sharply.

Rafe Bannerman regarded him impassively.

'You are drunk, Worsthorne. Go to bed.'

Luke swung round, his lip curling in a snarl.

'You are not master here yet, Bannerman!' he hiccupped. 'Perhaps you never will be. I shall stay here until *I* choose to go!' He slopped more brandy into his glass and gave the company a mocking salute as he walked unsteadily across the room. Mrs Worsthorne followed him, her cheeks flushed with indignation.

'Luke that is enough, I say!' She got no further. Luke shook off her restraining arm and as he did so he lost his balance and toppled forward into the fire. His head crashed against the stone mantel, the glass dropped from his hand to smash on the fender and Luke fell, unconscious, on to the flames.

★   ★   ★

Mrs Worsthorne screamed. Rafe Bannerman swiftly pushed her to one side and stepped forward to pull the lifeless form off the coals, but not before Luke's left sleeve was well alight. He dropped Luke to the floor and snatched up a cushion to smother the flames. Then he began carefully peeling the charred cloth from the arm.

'Quickly ma'am. Fetch me cold water and some rags: we must cool the burned skin.' She ran quickly out of the room, calling for Ditton. She returned moments later with a large pitcher, while the butler followed with strips of clean sheeting which Mr Bannerman proceeded to drench in the cold water and wrap around the burned limb. With Ditton's help he lifted Luke on to the sofa, and Mrs Worsthorne placed a small table beside him to support the injured arm.

'We must keep replacing the dressings,' muttered Mr Bannerman, rising to his feet. 'It is important that we reduce the heat from the burn as quickly as possible.'

'I took the liberty of sending Thomas out to the ice-house, sir,' offered Ditton. 'I thought ice might help the cooling.'

'An excellent idea,' nodded Mr Bannerman. He smiled at Mrs Worsthorne. 'Don't fret, ma'am. We must be thankful it was only his arm that is burned and with such prompt action Luke will make a good recovery, with only a little scarring.'

The young man stirred, muttering, and his fond mama knelt beside him, tenderly brushing the fair hair from his pallid face.

'Hush, love. You have burned your arm and must lie still for a little while.'

'Must I?' he blinked at her. 'It hurts damnably.'

'I know, my dear, but you must bear it a little longer. Thomas is gone to fetch ice to put on it and that will take away the pain.'

Luke frowned and tried to rise but fell back, groaning.

'Be still, love, hush now,' cried Mrs Worsthorne, pressing him back on to the sofa.

Luke's face contorted with pain then with a shuddering sigh he sank back against the cushions and lay still.

'He has fainted,' declared Mrs Worsthorne.

'That is for the best, I think. He is in considerable pain.' Mr Bannerman put a fresh damp cloth over the arm while Mrs Worsthorne watched him, wringing her hands.

'Oh where is Thomas? Ditton, do you go and find . . . oh thank goodness here he is!' She broke off as the door opened then gave a little scream as the footman appeared, a bucket of ice in one hand while his other arm supported the shivering and bedraggled figure of Verity Shore.

15

'Oh my poor child, what has happened to you?' Mrs Worsthorne rushed forward and with a sob Verity fell into her arms.

'She — she was locked in the ice-house,' stammered Thomas, handing the ice bucket to the butler.

'What!' Mrs Worsthorne stared in horror at Verity's straw-covered gown. She guided the sobbing girl to a chair, urgently ordering the butler to bring a little brandy.

It was some time before explanations could be offered. Mr Bannerman was busy packing ice around Luke's arm and Mrs Worsthorne hovered over Verity, coaxing her to take little sips of the brandy. Verity was shivering uncontrollably and Ditton was despatched to fetch a blanket.

Mr Bannerman glanced up. 'My coat is over there, use that.'

'No!' Verity clung to Mrs Worsthorne, trembling. 'No, not that!' she stared at Rafe Bannerman, her eyes dark with fear and the gentleman started to his feet.

'Miss Shore — what is it, what has happened?'

She shrank back in her chair. 'Don't come near me!'

He stopped, frowning, and Mrs Worsthorne put her arm about Verity's shaking shoulders.

'My poor child, drink your brandy, there's a good girl; it will restore you. Then you can tell us what has happened.'

Obediently Verity sipped at the spirit. Ditton returned with a thick blanket which he placed tenderly about her shoulders while Thomas was making his explanation to Mr Bannerman.

'I took the lantern and went out to the ice-house, as Mr Ditton asked me to do, sir, and I sees Will Barber just coming back from the fair so I asks him to come with me. We always goes in twos if we can, you see, because it's a fair drop down to the ice this year, and it's better if there's someone to hold the ladder. Well, we opens up the door and I puts the ladder down ready to climb down to the ice when I hears this moaning. Frightened the wits out o' me, I can tell you, and then by the light o' the lantern I sees Miss Shore curled up in the straw! Half dead she is with cold, so Will and I helps her up the ladder and brings her into the house.'

'And the ice-house doors were closed, you say?'

'Aye sir. Both of 'em. And bolted, too.'

'Thank you, Thomas.' Mr Bannerman nodded dismissal to the footman, who followed Ditton out of the room. As the door closed upon them, the gentleman shook his head. 'So it could not have been an accident.'

Revived by the brandy, Verity raised her eyes to stare at him.

'You know very well it was not!' She clung to Mrs Worsthorne. 'He tricked me. I — I followed him from the gardens and wh-when we reached the ice house he — he threw me on to the ice and shut me in.'

She buried her face in Mrs Worsthorne's skirts, and that good lady gasped.

'You must be mistaken, child.' She looked appealingly at Mr Bannerman, who shook his head. He was staring at Verity, his black brows drawn together.

'I did not leave the office all afternoon.'

Verity raised her head again. She held out her hand, opening the fingers to display the crumpled silk handkerchief bearing Rafe Bannerman's bold initials in one corner.

'I saw you,' she said, her voice low and throbbing with anger. 'When Jed Gatley found the arrowhead under Delphi's saddle I would not believe it was you — I did not want to believe it was you! But now . . . there can be no mistake.'

'Verity — ' He reached out to her, but she

shrank away, trembling, and his hand fell. 'This is not the time to go into this.' He looked at Mrs Worsthorne. 'My presence here is disturbing Miss Shore. I will send Ditton and Thomas to take Luke up to his room and I will stay with him there. You might wish to send for the doctor in the morning, ma'am.' As he opened the door he cast a final, enigmatic glance at Verity huddled by the fire. 'Goodnight, my dear. You will not believe me, but I thank God you are safe.'

Verity closed her eyes, trying to control the shivering that racked her body while her fingers clung desperately to Mrs Worsthorne.

'He must go,' she whispered. 'I will not have him in this house!'

'But my love, he has just saved Luke from the most terrible suffering!'

'He tried to kill me, Megs!'

'I cannot believe it of Rafe,' cried Mrs Worsthorne in dismay. 'There is no reason . . . why should he want to harm you?'

'He — he wants Highclough, Megs. He wants Highclough, but not me!'

Mrs Worsthorne shook her head, disbelieving.

'No, love, surely — '

'Please, Megs!' Verity was adamant. 'Tell him he must go!'

'My dear child it is nearly midnight! You

cannot turn him out now! Besides, he is tending to Luke, and there is no one else who knows so well what to do . . . '

'As soon as it is light, then!'

The widow sighed and nodded.

'Very well. I will tell him first thing in the morning.'

'And g-give orders that Delphi is to be returned to Newlands. I will have nothing connected with Rafe Bannerman in this house; do you understand me, Megs?'

'Yes, yes, calm yourself, my dear. Now, here are Thomas and Ditton come to take Luke to his room. Careful now . . . put his arm across his chest, Thomas, that's it! And be careful not to jar him!'

Having supervised her son's removal, Mrs Worsthorne turned back to Verity, her kind face creased with anxiety as she looked at the figure huddled in the chair.

'It is time that we got you to bed, my love. We will make sure Ella has warmed your sheets for you.'

'And can you have a bed made up for her in my room, ma'am? I c-cannot be alone tonight.'

Mrs Worsthorne put her arm about her and helped Verity to her feet. 'To be sure we can, my love. We shall watch over you with the greatest care!'

* * *

Verity insisted on coming downstairs for dinner the following day, despite Mrs Worsthorne's protests. She was very pale, and the widow cried out in dismay at her appearance.

'My love, I feel sure you should have kept to your bed today, or at least allowed me to send Dr Haworth to look at you, when he had finished with Luke.'

Verity shook her head as she lowered herself carefully into a chair.

'Luke's falling into the fire could be explained by the fact that he was drunk. I fear the good doctor's suspicions would have been aroused if he had been called upon to attend me as well, and I have no wish to be the object of gossip and speculation! Don't look so anxious, Megs. I promise you I am merely a little bruised from the rough treatment I received yesterday, and I have done nothing more strenuous today than writing letters. How is Luke?' She changed the subject to one guaranteed to give Mrs Worsthorne's thoughts another turn.

'Still sleeping. Dr Haworth has prescribed laudanum to ease the pain.' She hesitated. 'He praised our attempts to cool the arm and says he does not expect Luke to suffer any loss of movement.'

'Thank heaven for that! As soon as he is well enough I need to talk to him about the estate accounts. I spent this afternoon looking through the ledgers but with little success. I fear he will think me quite dull-witted, for I could not understand a great deal of it!'

'It pains me to confess that Luke was ever an untidy scholar,' admitted his fond mama. 'Unlike Rafe, who keeps his books in excellent order.' She paused and cast an uncertain glance across the table. 'Verity — my love, have you reconsidered the events of yesterday?'

'You mean was I mistaken in accusing Rafe Bannerman of trying to kill me?' Verity sighed. 'It is not what I want to believe, in fact I thought . . . but I *saw* him, Megs!' Verity stared before her, such a look of despair in her face that Mrs Worsthorne's kind heart ached for her.

'My dear, there could be another explanation . . .'

'Oh, Megs, I know, and it has been gnawing away at me all day! It is possible that someone took his coat and hat and tricked me — in fact, the more I think of it the more I know it is possible, but who, Megs? Mr Bannerman has a reason for wanting me dead, for then he would inherit Highclough, but who else could it be? Who hates me enough to want me to die in such a fashion? If Luke had not been burned — ' She broke off, shuddering.

'So, my love, if you do not believe Master Rafe to be the culprit . . . '

'Why have I banished him from the house?' Verity spread her hands. 'A mixture of reasons, Megs, which I cannot explain, even to myself, but in the main . . . in the main because he accepts it! I accused him, Megs, and I thought he would refute it, I wanted him to tell me I was mistaken, to prove to me that he is innocent! Surely his very silence suggests his guilt?' She broke off, blinking away her tears.

'So what will you do now?'

'Do? I don't know yet. Highclough has given me some of my happiest memories . . . and the worst. Once I have attained my majority and the property is secure, I may go abroad for a while. Don't look so sad, Megs, it was not my intention to upset you! Let us think instead of what you will do when Luke no longer has to look after Highclough for me. You will have a new house to keep.'

'You mean at Sowerby? Yes, when Luke drove me over to see it last week I was pleasantly surprised. From his description I had feared we would be moving to a hovel, but it is quite a new property, and Ambrose gave orders for it to be fully refurbished not long before his death, so we shall be quite snug there.' She sighed. 'I only wish Luke was happier about it: he shows no interest in Sowerby. I fear leaving Highclough will be a wrench for him.'

A wry smile lifted the corners of Verity's mouth.

'It will be a wrench for me, too.'

★ ★ ★

With her birthday fast approaching, Verity began to take over more of the running of Highclough. Mrs Worsthorne was very happy to relinquish her housekeeping duties while she concentrated on nursing her son, whose accident had resulted in a fever. Unfortunately Miss Shore found that sorting linen and sketching in the shrubbery left her mind too much leisure to dwell on unpleasant memories, so she spent ever more of her time in the estate office. Gradually she began to bring some order to her cousin's haphazard system of working, but there were still many questions she could not answer and after several days of trying to make sense of the figures she made up her mind to talk to Luke. Mrs

Worsthorne did not appear at breakfast, so as soon as she had given her daily orders to Ditton and to Cook, Verity made her way upstairs. She reached Luke's door just as Mrs Worsthorne came out.

'How is he, Megs?'

That lady shook her head.

'Very fretful, my love. I have been sitting up with him for most of the night. The fever has lifted now, thank God, but it has left him weak, very weak. However, I have just given him laudanum and I hope now that he will sleep.'

'Then I will not disturb him.' Verity put her hand out. 'Poor Megs, you look exhausted. Do you go and lie down for a while.'

Megs went on her way and Verity lingered in the passage, looking out of the window. A low cloud hung over the moors, enveloping everything in a grey half-light. She was wondering if she should make one more attempt to understand the accounts when a commotion below reached her, and she hurried downstairs to find Rafe Bannerman on the doorstep and a harassed Ditton barring his entry into the house.

'What is going on here?' Her icy tone brought all eyes towards her. The butler greeted her appearance with relief.

'Ah Madam, you said — that is — I have

been trying to explain to the gentleman, that you gave orders — '

Mr Bannerman cut across his tangled explanations.

'Miss Shore, I came here expressly to talk to you. Pray give me just five minutes of your time.'

She hesitated and the gentleman's hard eyes narrowed.

'Afraid I might do you injury in your own house, ma'am?'

An angry flush mounted her cheeks. She drew herself up.

'Of course not. You will come into the morning-room, if you please.'

He gave his hat and gloves to Ditton and followed her, shutting the door of the morning-room firmly against the interested servants hovering in the great hall.

He walked to the window and stood for a moment, silently gazing out. He was still wearing his driving coat, and for a moment Verity saw not the shadowy figure enticing her into danger, but the saviour who had rescued her from a life of drudgery at Cromford. She thrust the memory aside.

'Well, sir?' she spoke coldly. 'I can give you five minutes, nothing more.'

He turned to look at her. 'You are convinced I tried to kill you?'

'Yes — no. I don't know. Yes!' she ended defiantly.

'And will you tell me how I performed this act?'

'You know very well what happened!'

'No, tell me.' She shook her head, and he said with sudden exasperation, 'Surely a condemned man has a right to know just what he is supposed to have done?'

'You know very well! You came to the shrubbery and bade me follow you.'

'I spoke to you?'

'Yes!'

'In my own voice?'

'In — in a whisper.'

'Go on.'

'I — I followed you into the passage of the ice-house. The inner door was open and — and you threw me down into the pit.'

'What was I wearing?'

'That very coat, and your hat.'

'I suppose it would do no good to suggest that anyone could have taken my coat from its peg?'

She clenched her fists.

'The outer door was locked! No, sir! You convinced me once before that you were innocent. I will not be tricked again.' She paused, hoping he would contradict her and when he remained silent she added, 'I could not be mistaken, I was too close to you.'

'As close as this?' In two strides he was before her, his hands gripping her shoulders. With a cry she recoiled and he instantly let her go. Trembling, she clutched at a chair back for support. He stepped back. 'Verity —'

'Get out!' She glared at him, knowing in her heart she wanted him to argue with her, to demand that she listen to him.

An angry pulse throbbed in his cheek as he returned her stare. Then he sighed, and rubbed one hand across his eyes.

'Very well. Sir Ambrose's affairs are in good order now. Reedley has all the necessary papers and he will be able to work from that . . .'

Disappointment seared through her, and with it an unreasoning anger.

'I have written to him.' She looked away. 'I have also sent him a sealed letter describing the attempts upon my life: if I am prevented from taking up my inheritance on my birthday he is instructed to open the letter and act upon it as he sees fit.'

He bit back an oath.

'Why not call in the magistrate now and let us get to the bottom of this mystery?' he demanded. 'Give me the chance to clear my name.'

'When you are so well connected in this area, and the magistrate is a close acquaintance?' Her lip curled. 'He might prove your innocence to his own satisfaction, but never to mine!'

'Very well, madam. I understand you and I shall leave now, but for God's sake take care, Verity! *I* would never harm you, but there is someone here who wants you dead!'

She turned away, refusing to acknowledge his words. There was a long silence then, just when she thought she could bear it no longer, she heard him leave the room.

★   ★   ★

Verity sank on to a chair and dropped her head in her hands. He had put forward no argument against the proof of her own eyes. His only defence was that someone might have taken his hat and coat, but she knew the servants had all been at the May Fair, and she herself had checked that the rear door was locked. A depression settled over her spirits, and it lifted only fractionally when she found Luke was well enough to join them for dinner. He was very pale, but smilingly apologized for joining them without his jacket.

'Mama insists I keep the arm in its sling for another day!'

Verity was glad of the diversion, and found the effort of entertaining her cousin and coaxing him to eat lightened her own spirits. As the covers were removed she raised her glass to him.

'I think you managed the meal quite creditably, Cousin, considering you had the use of only one arm.'

He returned the salute.

'Thank you. Tomorrow I intend to leave off the sling, get into my coat and go to Halifax.'

Mrs Worsthorne was reaching for a sweetmeat but at his words she paused.

'Will you ride out so soon?'

'No, no, Mama. William shall drive me in the gig. Don't fret, dearest.'

She was not proof against his winning smile and her eyes softened as she regarded her son.

'How can I help it, my love, when you are so headstrong?'

'Nonsense, I have been a very good patient. Besides, I have to choose a present to celebrate our cousin's birthday.' He turned to Verity. 'On Thursday next you will be one and twenty. How does that suit you, Cousin?'

Verity glanced up, observing that the servants had quit the room.

'It suits me well, I think, although I have my reservations. I shall be glad to have it settled, and know exactly what I own. Which reminds me, Luke. I saw Brigg's name in the account books when I was going through them the other day, and there were a few other points I do not understand.'

'By all means, Cousin. We will go through it all tomorrow. By the by, are the other papers in order? Mama told me about Rafe . . . '

Verity put up her hand, her pain too raw to admit discussion.

'I understand Mr Reedley has everything he needs to complete the transfer. It will be ready to sign over to me on the day.'

'Will you let me go with you?'

'Thank you, Cousin, but no. Megs is coming with me — pray do not look so serious, Luke, we will take a footman, and a groom upon the box. I know the dangers of travelling unprotected.'

He looked suddenly serious. 'You fear another attack?'

'No.' Verity put up her chin. 'I have taken certain . . . measures to ensure my safety.'

Luke pushed his chair back.

'Mama tells me you have forbidden Bannerman to come here. How will he take that, I wonder?'

227

Verity tossed her head.

'I neither know nor care!'

'Well, I do care!' declared Mrs Worsthorne, with uncharacteristic force. 'It saddens me to see this rift between the families. I have always valued Rafe Bannerman, and his actions in pulling you so swiftly from the fire — ' She broke off to hunt for her handkerchief.

Her son dismissed her words with a wave of his hand.

'A little thing, Mama, compared to his treatment of our cousin!'

Verity bent her clear gaze upon him.

'You do not doubt it was Mr Bannerman who tried to kill me?'

'No, Cousin, for I have always mistrusted him. Sir Ambrose thought the world of Rafe Bannerman, treated him like a son once Evelyn was gone, but I always saw him for what he was. I shall be glad to know he is no longer allowed on our land. It has always rankled to see him riding around Highclough as if he owns it!'

Verity looked away from the triumphant light in his eyes. She felt rather sick. Luke poured himself more wine.

'No, we shall go on much more comfortably now, Cousin, and we can forget those foolish ideas of building a spinning mill in Beech Clough.'

'Actually, I have decided to go ahead with that.' Verity gave her attention to selecting a sweetmeat from the dish in front of her. 'I think the mill is too important to the area, so I have told Mr Reedley to discuss it with those involved and to draw up the papers: we shall begin building this summer!'

16

'Well, Miss Shore, may I be the first to congratulate you? You are now a woman of considerable means!' Mr Reedley shook Verity's hand, his gentle grey eyes twinkling. He indicated the pile of documents on the table. 'You will want to take these back to Highclough with you.'

'Thank you. You have sent my papers to Mr Oldroyd?'

'Yes. The plans are already drawn up for the mill, and he will bring them over to show you in a few days.'

'You made it quite, quite plain that I want no contact with Mr Bannerman?'

'I did. Mr Oldroyd thought it a little irregular, but he is quite happy to co-operate.'

She flushed slightly. 'And . . . Mr Bannerman?'

'He too has indicated his willingness to agree. Mr Oldroyd and myself will act as intermediaries in all business matters. There will be no necessity for you to meet Mr Bannerman, unless you wish it.'

'Thank you.' She turned to the documents and saw her letter to Mr Reedley resting on the top. Following her glance, Mr Reedley said quietly, 'I have followed your instructions, Miss Shore. The second letter has not been opened. It can now be destroyed, if you so wish.'

'Yes, I think so. There is no danger now. In fact, I — I wrote them in a fit of anger: I doubt if there was ever any danger from that quarter.' She turned to Mrs Worsthorne. 'Perhaps you would wait for me in the carriage, Megs?'

As the widow bustled out, Mr Reedley picked up the letters and dropped them on to the fire, where the paper quickly blackened and curled away to ash. Verity sighed as she watched the flames.

'Mr Reedley, I am minded to go away for a while. Can you find me a good manager to look after the estate until I return?'

'A manager?' the old man looked startled. 'Miss Shore, I had thought — '

'I know,' she interrupted him. 'I have grown to love Highclough, sir, but at the present time I do not know if I can bear to live there.'

'Perhaps Mr Worsthorne would be willing to carry on . . . '

'No. There are reasons why I do not wish that.'

Mr Reedley nodded slowly. 'Very well. How

long do you plan to be away?'

'Six months, perhaps a year. I do not know.'

Mr Reedley regarded her closely.

'We will be sorry to lose you again so soon, Miss Shore, but yes, I will find a suitable person to run the estate, and I will send him along to you.'

★ ★ ★

'Well, Verity Shore.' Mrs Worsthorne settled herself more comfortably into the carriage. 'It is done: you are now mistress of Highclough!'

'Yes. How strange it is, Megs! And I cannot help feeling that I have usurped you!'

'Fiddle, child. In fact, I am looking forward to living at Sowerby. The house is quite close to the town, you see. When Mr Worsthorne and I were first married we lived on the edge of a small town, and I did enjoy being able to visit my neighbours whenever I wished. From Sowerby it is a gentle stroll into the village, instead of having to order the carriage as we do at Highclough.'

'Then I wish you joy in your new home.' She smiled, smothering a sigh as she turned away.

She would miss Megs's cheerful company. Verity gazed out of the window as the carriage rattled out of the town, the road following the curve of the hills with the high moors reaching to the sky on one side and a thickly wooded valley falling away on the other. The leaden clouds reflected her mood but Verity did not want her companion to guess at her low spirits. Megs had arranged a special dinner in her honour for the evening, inviting the vicar and his wife as well as two of her new business partners, Mr Williams and his wife and Mr and Mrs Oldroyd to join them. Verity was well aware that until a week ago Mr Bannerman's name had also been on the list. She swallowed hard, determined she would not give in to this melancholy.

As she stared out of the window her attention was caught by a solitary rider crossing the moors. Her heart leapt to her throat: surely there was no mistaking that upright figure. She closed her eyes, telling herself her mind was playing tricks, but when she opened them again the rider was a little closer, and she could make out the detail of his high-crowned hat and the almost white coat with its flapping shoulder capes. For one wild moment she wondered if he would stop the coach and demand to talk to her, convince her of his innocence. The thought occurred only to be dismissed, for the horse and rider halted at some distance from the road and as she watched, a second rider appeared and she realized that Mr Bannerman had been waiting for him. Verity stared, blinked, then stifled a cry. The second rider was touching his forelock to Mr Bannerman in a gesture she could not mistake: it was Brigg, the former groom at Highclough.

17

Never had Verity felt so low. Upon their return from Halifax she escaped to her room, declaring that she wanted to rest before dinner, but even lying on her bed there was no respite from her thoughts, for when she closed her eyes the image of Rafe Bannerman was imprinted on her eyelids, and the damning vision of his meeting with Brigg.

At dinner Verity's poise and serene smile were unshakeable: she responded to all questions calmly and if she allowed Luke to fill her glass more often than usual, no one commented. It was, after all, her birthday. With the moon not rising until after midnight, Mrs Worsthorne had risked being thought provincial and arranged an early dinner so that their guests could return to their homes before the daylight had completely disappeared, and it was with relief that Verity returned to the drawing-room once the final carriage had pulled away. Luke ordered Ditton to bring the brandy and Mrs Worsthorne cast an anxious glance at her son. However, Luke appeared to be in high good humour and determined to please. He challenged Verity to a game of backgammon and afterwards surprised his mother by reading to her from one of her favourite poets.

'How delightful it has been to have you with us tonight.' Mrs Worsthorne smiled fondly at her son. 'I don't know when I was last so well entertained!'

'It was indeed a wonderful evening,' agreed Verity. 'Thank you, Megs. Goodness, it is nearly midnight! If you will excuse me I think I shall retire, it has been such a long day.'

'But surely, Cousin, you will not go yet!' cried Luke. 'Let Mama go on to bed, but give me another chance to have my revenge at backgammon.'

Verity smiled but shook her head.

'That pleasure must wait for another evening, Cousin. I long for my bed.'

He dropped to his knees beside her chair.

'But you have never seen the full moon rising over the moors. The clouds have disappeared now and soon the moon will be in view: step outside with me, it would be the perfect end to your birthday!'

She laughed at him.

'Luke! There will be other moons. I think I can last a little longer without the experience!'

236

She bade him good night and followed Mrs Worsthorne upstairs.

★ ★ ★

As soon as she had removed her gown and put on her silk wrap, Verity dismissed her maid and sat before her mirror, brushing out her hair. She glanced down at the miniature of her father that she kept on her dressing-table. It occurred to her that the restlessness that now possessed her was inherited: after all, her father had longed to go to sea and sacrificed so much to do so. Perhaps travel would help to push aside the unhappiness that seemed to hang about her. She would settle her affairs at Highclough and go to Portsmouth, and from there she would go abroad. Travel was not without its dangers of course, especially while the country remained at war with France, but there were other countries, and surely amongst her father's naval colleagues there would be one who could advise her, or even act as her courier. She remembered a retired naval man who had been their neighbour in Portsmouth: she would write to him and ask his advice. She began to compose a letter in her mind, but was interrupted by an urgent knock at her door.

Luke was waiting for her, a single candlestick in his hand.

'Cousin, come quickly!'

'What is it? Megs — is she ill?'

He caught her wrist. 'There is no time to lose — quickly, the south passage.'

'But what on earth would Megs be doing there now?'

He did not reply but set off down the stairs, almost dragging her with him.

'Luke, Luke, what is this?'

'Hush. I will explain soon enough. Just follow me, Cousin!'

★   ★   ★

The house was in darkness and they crossed the hall with only the light from Luke's candle to help them: it sent grotesque shadows dancing around the walls. Verity clutched her wrap about her and noted with some surprise that Luke had exchanged his soft evening pumps for leather top boots which thudded noisily across the floor.

'Luke, what is this, why are you dressed for riding?' Verity hung back as they entered the office passage. Luke put down the candle and pulled her forward.

'Come to the door and you will see.'

As they approached the outer door it

swung open, and a stocky figure stepped into the passage.

'Brigg!'

Verity gasped with surprise, but in a second Brigg sprang forward, clapping one hand over her mouth.

'Quick master, gag her!' he hissed.

Luke produced a scarf which he roughly tied around her face. Verity stared at him, her eyes wide with fear and anger. He gave her a twisted smile.

'Forgive me, Cousin. I shall remove the gag as soon as we are safe from here.' He took her arms. 'I have her now, Brigg. Bring the horses.'

Moments later, she found herself perched up before Luke on his rangy black hunter. She struggled, vainly trying to free herself.

'Be still, Cousin. I know this is uncomfortable but I can't risk a carriage. Neither can we leave by the main gates.'

Pressed close against Luke, Verity had no idea of their direction as they rode out of the stable yard and across the fields. The sky was clear but the moon had not yet risen and only the faintest shadow indicated the line between land and sky. A keen wind cut through Verity's thin wrap and she shivered. Luke's arm tightened.

'Afraid? There is no need to be, if you

will only be sensible.'

She smelled the brandy on his breath and turned her head away in disgust. They rode on, with only the occasional cry of a fox or the whirring of a nightjar to disturb the silence. Verity closed her eyes. If Luke would relax his iron-like grip she could perhaps jump down and escape, or at the very least pull off the gag and scream for help. However, no opportunity occurred and after they had been travelling for some time Luke spoke again.

'Look, Cousin, over there. Did I not say it would be a magnificent moon tonight?'

She opened her eyes and lifted her head. In the east the full moon had risen, and hung now like a blood-red ball just clear of the horizon. In its pale light she could see that they were crossing the moors, with the black rocky outcrop of Bridestones looming ahead of them. Luke reached up to remove the scarf from her mouth.

'I think we can dispense with that. You can make as much noise as you like now, there is no one here to come to your aid.'

'Luke what is happening, why are you doing this?'

'You will know soon enough.'

Panic constricted her throat, and she fought to speak calmly.

'Luke, listen to me! It will do you no good to kill me, I drew up a new will today: if I die, the estate is to be broken up and sold. Highclough will not remain in the family.'

He looked down at her.

'Kill you? I've no intention of killing you, Verity.' He nodded towards Bridestones. 'I have arranged another little party for you, my love.'

Looking up, Verity became aware of yellow lights flickering between the stones. She forced herself to be calm.

'What madness is this? I am not dressed, Luke. Take me home.'

'Not until we are wed, my dear.'

'What? You are being nonsensical. We cannot be married here.'

'Why not? Locals have been plighting their troth here for years. And it will be quite legal. I have the special licence in my pocket and the priest is genuine . . . after a fashion.'

Verity gripped her hands together to stop them from shaking.

'Cousin, let us go back, we can discuss this in the morning.'

'There is nothing to discuss. You must marry me.' He pulled a flask from his pocket, took a long draught and held it out to Verity.

'Brandy,' he said. 'Take it, it will help you to forget the cold.'

Fearing he would force her to comply, Verity took the flask and raised it to her lips, pretending to drink.

'Is this why you kept Brigg on my accounts? To help you kidnap me?'

'I told you, Cousin, Brigg is a loyal servant. I could not dismiss him.'

They were almost at the Bridestones and she could hear voices and raucous laughter echoing out into the night.

'We do not have to be married this way, Cousin.' She handed back the flask. 'Take me home, Luke. We could have the banns called and be married at Derringden Church. Think how your mama would like that!'

He laughed harshly. 'You think me a fool? You will not marry me unless I force you to it. I did hope that if you believed Rafe a villain you might agree to marry me, but I could see it wouldn't work. And you are still determined to build that damned mill.'

'But this will solve nothing!'

'Now there you are wrong, my dear. Once we are married, Highclough becomes mine: there will be no mills on my land.'

Anger flared in her eyes.

'You disappoint me, Luke. I should have thought you would approve of my plans; the profits would help to pay back some of the money you have been leeching from

Highclough all these years!'

He looked down at her, grinning.

'So you discovered that, did you? Clever girl.'

'When you were laid up in your room I had the opportunity to study the books in more detail than you would allow me. I soon realized that your untidy habits were a cover to distract me from the flaws in your accounts: payments to servants who did not exist, rents entered at rates lower than the tenancy agreements. What did you do with the money, Luke? Gambling? Brandy?'

He gave a harsh laugh. 'Aye, and my tailor, too. You cannot conceive the cost of being well dressed.'

'And the estate at Sowerby is not enough: you must have Highclough too.'

'It belongs to me!' cried Luke. 'How could you understand, you have been here less than six months! Since I was a child I have worked on this land, striving to make it pay for itself. I was like a son to Ambrose — more so than his own children — your father Charles was only interested in the sea, and Evelyn, well, he did not love it as I do. When he broke his neck I thought Ambrose would make me his heir — it is what he should have done!'

'And — and was Evelyn's death an accident, Luke?'

Luke gave a short laugh. 'Lord yes. The fool over-faced his horse.'

They were riding beneath the rocky cliff and his words echoed eerily back around them. Brigg brought his horse alongside his master.

'We are almost there, sir.'

Verity's lips curled. 'And just who do you serve, Brigg? I saw you talking to Rafe Bannerman on the moor today. Is he involved in this too?'

She felt Luke grow tense. He turned his head to stare at his servant.

'Is this true?'

The groom sniffed. 'I was making my way to Highclough this afternoon when Bannerman came across my path, but I fobbed him off.'

'Aye, Rafe Bannerman's a fool!' sneered Worsthorne. 'I should have liked to see him hanged for your murder, Cousin, but that plan did not work.'

Verity raised her head. 'What plan?'

'To kill you, my dear.'

'Master.'

Luke ignored Brigg's growled warning: Verity thought he sounded pleased to be able to tell her what he had done.

'It was fortunate that my first attempt failed. If the chimney stone had killed you,

Highclough would have gone to Rafe, and I would have lost everything.'

'*You* pushed the stone from the roof?'

'It required very little effort, my dear. You will remember Mama complaining of the damp on the bedroom wall, I went up to check the roof and when I saw you below in the shrubbery the opportunity was too good to resist. Of course *then* I did not know that Highclough would go to Bannerman!'

Fear trickled down Verity's spine.

'And the barb under Delphi's saddle?'

'Master, no more!' hissed Brigg.

'Quiet, damn you!' snarled Luke. 'What does it matter if I tell her everything? A wife cannot testify against her husband. Where was I? Oh yes, the arrowhead. That was Brigg's clumsy attempt to dispose of you and implicate Bannerman. But he did not follow it up, and you survived with barely a scratch.' He drank again from the flask, enjoying the recital of his cleverness. 'Of course that made Rafe suspicious, and I thought I should not have another chance to implicate him. I *had* to do so, you see, because if you died, and Rafe was convicted of your murder, then Highclough would go to the next in line, my mother. My plan would have succeeded, too, if I had not fallen into that damned fire.'

'Then it wasn't Rafe . . . but I saw him

— he spoke to me!'

Luke laughed again, a wild note in his voice.

'Could anyone be so careless? He always leaves his coat in the passage, I have often seen it when I have returned to the house.'

'But the passage door was locked, Luke.'

'There is a spare key in the stable so that I can come and go as I please without Mama and Ditton fussing over me! That day I had just ridden back from Halifax and was in the stable when you came round the back of the house. I saw you, flirting with Rafe through the window! I knew then what I had to do. We are of a height, Rafe and I, so it was easy to put on his coat and hat and walk through the gardens, and you followed, thinking he was leading you somewhere private where you could continue your love-making!' His lip curled. 'There was a handkerchief in his pocket. I made sure it went into the ice-pit with you. When they found that with your body, they would know he had locked you in — and how could he deny it?'

So Rafe was innocent! Despite her present danger she felt her spirits lift. A sigh escaped her and she felt Luke's arm tighten across her chest, squeezing the breath from her.

'But you were on my conscience, my dear,' Luke continued. 'I went down to the village, but couldn't get you out of my mind, no matter how much brandy I took! I've grown damned fond of you, Cousin, so this way is better for both of us — you will live, and I will have Highclough.' Verity could not prevent the despairing cry escaping from her, and she felt Luke's cheek rest briefly against her hair. 'Now, now, my love. No tears on our wedding night!'

They passed between the two entrance stones into the rocky enclosure. Torches had been jammed into crevices in the rock to light the area, and Verity saw that a number of rough-looking men were waiting for them. One was dressed in ragged cleric's robes. He looked uncomfortable, but he had a bottle in his hand from which he was constantly refreshing himself.

A stocky figure walked forward, a toothless grin splitting his face.

'So this is the Highclough lady.' His eyes observed her thin wrap. 'And dressed for bed already!'

'Aye, Joe. Hold her for me while I dismount.'

Verity was pushed roughly from the saddle and found herself pinioned in the man's arms. She struggled as he leered at her, the stench of beer and onions on his breath making her retch. Brigg led the horses away and Luke pulled Verity back into his arms. He beckoned to the cleric.

'Well, Parson, here is my bride. Let's make a start.'

'Aye,' cried Joe with cackling laugh. 'Then we can all enjoy the wedding night.'

Verity shrank closer to Luke as the men crowded around.

'What-what does he mean?' she whispered.

Luke pointed to the rocky shelf at the far side of the enclosure.

'Our wedding bed, my dear. I need witnesses that the marriage has been consummated, just in case you try to have it annulled.'

She paled. 'You can't mean it! You could not be so cruel to me.'

He shrugged. 'What's the difference if I take you here or at Highclough?'

'No!' Verity struggled, but could not escape Luke's iron grip. His fingers dug into her skin through the thin silk wrap while around her the men's brutal laughter echoed between the stones.

'Sir,' the priest remonstrated anxiously, 'I really do not think — '

'I didn't bring you here to think!' snarled Luke. 'Get on with it before the little wildcat wrenches my arms off.'

Verity struggled harder.

'No, no! I will not! You cannot make me!'

'Brigg, give her the brandy!'

At Luke's barked command, Brigg approached. With one hand he gripped Verity's hair and pulled back her head while with the other he tipped the contents of a bottle down her throat. She had no idea how much of the fiery liquid she swallowed, but as Brigg raised his hand again she shook her head.

'Luke, no more — please, no more!'

Luke signalled to the groom to stand back.

'So, will you be sensible now? Good. Come then, let's finish this.'

Verity watched as the vicar stepped forward, holding a Bible between his shaking hands. By the flaring torchlight the nightmare ceremony proceeded. As the brandy took effect Verity's eyelids drooped and she leaned against her cousin. The priest droned on, she heard his questions and made no answer, but the ceremony continued. Luke forced a ring on to her finger and she gazed at it, too drowsy to care what was happening.

' . . . you are now man and wife!'

The men around her gave a drunken cheer. Luke lifted her hand so that the light reflected on the heavy gold band.

'So, now you are my wife, and Highclough

is mine!' Luke laughed and gave her a rough kiss.

'And you know as well as I that this sham marriage is unlawful!' The words rang out around the stones. Verity's head jerked up. Rafe Bannerman stood in the entrance, his hands dug into the pockets of his white coat, which gleamed against the black night behind him. Will Barber and two other men stepped out of the darkness to stand at his shoulder.

'A defrocked priest and a drugged bride?' Mr Bannerman's lip curled. 'I gave you more credit, Worsthorne!' His hard glance flickered over the gathering. 'And you have brought your gambling cronies to help celebrate your nuptials? How touching, but I think we can dispense with their services.' He lifted one hand, drawing a horse pistol from the pocket of his coat. 'Vickery, Pecket and the rest of you — I know you all. You would be advised to go back to Derringden, and keep your heads down for a while if you do not want to suffer for this night's work.'

A silence had fallen over the company, and the men began to back away from Luke, some slipping between the stones to disappear into the night. Rafe Bannerman turned his attention back to the little group in the centre.

'It is finished, Luke,' he spoke quietly. 'Let her go.'

With a snarl Luke stepped back, pulling Verity with him.

'We made our vows, and there are witnesses to the fact!' He glanced about him, but most of the men had now gone, and the cleric had retreated against one wall, whimpering.

'Quiet!' screamed Luke. He turned back to look at Rafe Bannerman, and his wild eyes came to rest upon Will Barber.

'Will, come and aid me. I am master of Highclough now. You are employed by me!'

Mr Bannerman shook his head.

'Correction, Will is in *my* employ. Gabriel Gatley is an old friend of mine, and claimed Will for his nephew: I knew you would not take him on if you thought he had anything to do with me, but I needed someone to watch you. I'm only sorry that he spent May Day at the fair when he thought you safe in Halifax. If he had seen you return we might have saved Miss Shore an uncomfortable time in the ice-pit.'

Luke chewed his lip, looking about him. Only Brigg and two of his cronies remained, but they were both large men with cruel, battered faces and they looked eager to fight.

Rafe watched him, his face impassive.

'Let her go, Luke,' he said again.

'The devil I will! Fifty guineas to each of you to hold Bannerman and his men until I have made sure of my bride! Brigg, show 'em the way!'

As Brigg and his accomplices advanced upon Rafe Bannerman, Luke dragged Verity towards the stone shelf. Looking up into his face, she saw it was transfigured with rage, the eyes alight with a maniacal gleam. Knowing he was beyond reason, Verity dug in her heels, determined to fight every inch of the way as Luke pulled her across the floor. Losing patience, he picked her up and carried her to the stone embrasure where he threw her down on to the stone slab and climbed on top of her. She kicked and struggled, turning her head when he tried to kiss her. A shot rang out and in the guttering torchlight she saw Rafe Bannerman wrestling with Brigg. The advantage in height and weight was with Mr Bannerman, but the groom was a brawler and he was using all his strength to try to gouge out his opponent's eyes. For an instant Verity forgot her own predicament as she watched in horror while the black, ragged fingernails curled within an inch of Rafe Bannerman's face and in that moment Luke bore down upon her with a triumphant cry. She felt the weight of his body crushing her into the stone and she could do nothing to hold him off, her arms beating uselessly against his back. She swept her hand over the rocky shelf, grazing her knuckles on the rough wall. Then her fingers touched a loose rock. She scrabbled and strained to grasp it, all the while aware of Luke's breath on her neck, his hands pulling aside the thin wrap. With a desperate cry she squirmed beneath him, shifting her position very slightly, but it was enough. Her fingers curled about the stone and she brought her arm up in an arc then dashed the stone down upon his head with all her might. Luke slumped down on her and she found herself trapped beneath the dead weight of his unconscious body. With one last effort she pushed him aside and he tumbled to the floor.

★ ★ ★

Gasping, Verity sat up and with trembling hands pulled her silk wrap close about her. The enclosure was quiet now, with only the wind sighing softly around the stones. She tried to steady her breathing and to control the shudders that racked her body. Rafe Bannerman was coming towards her; he was breathing heavily, his white coat covered in

253

dirt and there was blood trickling from his lip. Verity watched him approach and crossed her arms tightly around her: she wanted to fly into his arms, yet perversely she was afraid she would recoil from his touch. He halted, and drew out his handkerchief to wipe the blood from his mouth. He looked at the body at her feet. 'You appear to have managed very well without my help, Miss Shore.'

She gave a shaky laugh. 'I did not realize I was so resourceful.' She tried to stand but her legs were so weak she was obliged to lean against the rock. Rafe dropped to his knees beside Luke.

'Is — is he dead?' she whispered.

'No, unconscious. Will is securing Brigg and his cronies now. My men will fetch a carriage to take all of them to the lock-up in Halifax.' He rose. 'You are trembling.'

'It is the cold.' She tried to stop her voice from shaking. 'I am really not dressed for the outdoors.'

The corners of his mouth lifted.

'No. I can see that.' He slipped out of his coat. 'Here, put this around you.'

She allowed him to throw the coat over her shoulders but his hands did not linger, and he made no move to touch her, merely stood looking down at her, his hard, unfathomable gaze searching her face. Then he held out one hand towards her, softly murmuring her name.

Slowly, she put out her hand and, as her fingers found his, her iron resolve deserted her. With a sob she fell towards him and he pulled her into his arms, holding her while she cried, his cheek resting gently against her hair. At last the tears subsided. She took his proffered handkerchief and began to wipe her eyes.

'Are you hurt?' he asked her, his voice harsh with anxiety. 'Did he . . . ?'

She shook her head. 'A little bruised, perhaps. Nothing worse.' She leaned against him again, sighing. 'Take me home, Rafe.'

★　★　★

Verity's journey back to Highclough was accomplished in the same manner as her outward one, yet her feelings could not have been more different. She sat across Mr Bannerman's saddle, wrapped in his coat and with her cheek resting comfortably against his chest, listening to the rhythmic thud of his heart. Above them the full moon was riding high and bathing the moors in a silver blue light. Feeling the strong arms about her, Verity felt very safe.

'Rafe, what will happen to them . . . to Luke?'

'They will all spend a few nights in the lock-up. Brigg and his accomplices will be charged with attempted murder and kidnap and Luke . . . well, attempted murder, abduction, attempted rape. These are serious offences, the penalties are severe.'

She shivered. 'Must it be so?'

He looked down at her. 'No. If you will not testify, the case cannot go ahead. Whatever you choose to do, be assured that Brigg and his cronies will not remain in the country. I will not allow it.'

The deadly resolve in his tone made her shiver.

'And . . . and Luke?' she murmured. 'I am thinking of poor Megs. She will be heartbroken.'

'Well, perhaps we should see what the doctors have to say, although I would see him hang for what he has done to you.'

She snuggled closer. 'Luke *is* being punished, Rafe. He cannot have Highclough, and he has lost his reason. We should not be unkind, when we have so much.'

'True.' His arms tightened about her. 'Look, you can see Highclough from this point.'

Verity raised her head. The house was in

256

darkness below them, the windows gleaming silver in the moonlight. She sighed, thinking of Megs and the sleeping household, as yet unaware of the night's activity.

'It looks so beautiful. I have grown to love it here.'

'And will you want to live at Highclough when we are married? Newlands would suit me better, but I can run the estate almost as easily from here.'

'Are we to be married?' she asked him, hiding a smile.

He gave a low growl. 'If you think I am going to spend the better part of a night rescuing you without some reward you are sadly mistaken. And then to be carrying you around the countryside, half-naked — '

'Rafe! I am perfectly respectable!'

'If you call that wisp of silk you are wearing respectable you are all about in your head!' he retorted.

She chuckled. 'Then you will have to marry me, to save my reputation. And I would be quite content to live at Newlands with you, as long as I can ride over the moors occasionally. Perhaps we could find a tenant for Highclough.'

'I think I might already have one for you: James Marsden, who will be overseeing the building of the mill at Beech Clough. He would need to be near at hand and he could easily direct matters from Highclough.'

'I could almost believe you had it all planned!' exclaimed Verity. She sighed and added mournfully, 'I see now that I have fallen into the clutches of an inveterate schemer.'

He reined in his horse and put a hand beneath her chin, tilting her face up until she was obliged to look at him. His eyes glinted in the moonlight.

'I knew when I first saw you at Cromford that you would be trouble!'

She struggled to free her arm from the folds of his voluminous coat, then she reached up, putting her fingers against his cheek.

'And I had the strangest feeling that you were my knight in shining armour!'

He shook his head at her. 'I am no Sir Galahad, my love.'

'No,' she said lovingly. 'You are blunt, overbearing, used to your own way and, if I remember correctly, odiously bad-tempered in the mornings!'

He was startled.

'A catalogue of faults indeed!'

With a low laugh she threw her arms about his neck.

'Yes,' she murmured, 'but without them just think how *dull* life would be!'